"Last night was an appetizer. My appetite is well and truly whetted. I want you in a bed, my bed, with all the hours of darkness ahead of us."

Color flooded her. Top to toe. Sienna knew it did. She could hear blood beating in her ears, feel it in her cheeks, the palms of her hands. Hell, even her ankles were blushing—her knees. Actually blushing. And it wasn't just embarrassment. It was the most words Rhys had strung together in the short time she'd known him, and she wished he hadn't because his voice was rich and deep and she couldn't help but listen—and be seduced. And she couldn't help but look at his mouth as it moved, and really those lips alone were seductive enough.

As for what he'd actually said…

The blush deepened. But she didn't have a chance in succeeding a second time. She'd have to get naked—and that she didn't want to do. She'd never forgotten the look on Neil's face. The way he'd recoiled. *Everything* would change.

What do you look for in a guy? Charisma. Sex appeal. Confidence. A body to die for. Looks that stand out from the crowd. Well, look no further—in Harlequin Presents® you've just found guys with all this—and more! And now that they've met the women in these novels, there is one thing on everyone's mind....

NIGHTS *of* PASSION

One night is never enough!

These guys know what they want and how they're going to get it!

Don't miss any of these hot stories, where sparky romance and sizzling passion are guaranteed!

Natalie Anderson

PLEASURED BY THE SECRET MILLIONAIRE

NIGHTS *of* PASSION

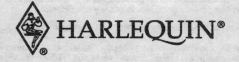

HARLEQUIN®

TORONTO • NEW YORK • LONDON
AMSTERDAM • PARIS • SYDNEY • HAMBURG
STOCKHOLM • ATHENS • TOKYO • MILAN • MADRID
PRAGUE • WARSAW • BUDAPEST • AUCKLAND

ISBN-13: 978-0-373-12834-1

PLEASURED BY THE SECRET MILLIONAIRE

First North American Publication 2009.

All about the author...
Natalie Anderson

Possibly the only librarian who got told off herself
for talking too much, **NATALIE ANDERSON**
decided writing books might be more fun than
shelving them—and boy, is it that. Especially
writing romance—it's the realization of a lifetime
dream kick-started by many an afternoon spent
devouring Grandma's Harlequin® novels.

She lives in New Zealand with her husband and
four gorgeous but exhausting children. Swing by
her Web site, www.natalie-anderson.com,
anytime—she'd love to hear from you.

For Bridge: over twenty-five years of best-friendship. Cool huh? I'm banking on at least sixty more…

And Kate: for all those Thursday mornings, awesome F&H adventures, yummy veggie dinners—not to mention the book on Peru! Thanks so much.

CHAPTER ONE

SYDNEY: sun, surf and shopping. All that was missing was the sex.

Sienna smiled as she crossed the beach, the soles of her feet tingling on the hot sand. Beautiful bodies decorated the shore and she cruised through them, winding her way back up to the footpath. Oh, yeah. If she ever went to a doctor again this would be the only prescription she'd pay attention to. One week of pure holiday—preparation time before her big adventure. Her first week where no one knew about her health or her history—the fresh beginning she'd been hanging out half her life for.

She paused to let a couple stroll by in front of her. Tried not to envy the way the woman oh-so-casually wore her teeny tiny triangles of material—aka her bikini. Crimson-red with shoe-string straps, it revealed more than it concealed and she had both the body and boldness to wear it. Sienna didn't have either. She didn't want the looks, the ill-concealed curiosity or pity. She didn't want the speculation full stop. Hence her throat-high top—even though it did cling and her miniskirt was more on the mini than the skirt side. And sure she'd spotted the odd sideways glance her way from a couple of men. As usual she'd shied away from them. She could never show her cleavage the way that woman did. Irritation increased her pace and she lectured her wavering confidence—must improve assertiveness quotient! How was she ever going to tick her way through her list of 'must achieve' activities if she couldn't even hold a stranger's gaze for more than a split second? How was that 'living in the moment'—her new motto?

Suddenly touched by melancholy she crossed the street, moving away from the beach and into the pub, club and café scene. She needed to buck up—wasn't it her New Year's resolution to live life to the max? Take no prisoners? Maybe she'd go dancing with the girls she'd met at the hostel the previous night. Full of adventure and fun, they'd be able to teach her a few tricks. At least she could hang on for the ride and watch. But that was what she was sick of—being the one on the sidelines, unable to participate because she wasn't allowed. Well, now she was allowed. And there was no one here to tell her she couldn't, wouldn't or shouldn't. But nor was there anyone to tell her she could, would or should either. She wished Lucy were here, her crazy friend who had all the gumption and the heart as well. The person who'd shown her some fun in spite of the restrictions all those years. But she'd had to come away alone—needing to prove to herself that she could do it. Because then she'd truly believe it and could insist others recognise it too.

She glanced at her watch. A bit after three p.m., the lunch crowd had moved on and everyone was back at work—except the tourists, travellers and holiday-makers like her. The restaurant and club a couple of blocks down from the hostel had its doors wide open—circulating air on the steamy Sydney day when the humidity was high and the thunderstorm approaching. She hoped it would happen soon; she wasn't used to the hard-to-breathe air.

Then she heard it. Boom, boom, hiss, boom, boom, hiss—

the unmistakable strike of stick on drum and cymbal. It stopped and then started again. Then she heard the twang of a rough chord on an electric guitar followed by a disembodied male voice. 'One, one. Two, t-t-t-two.'

Sound check.

Suddenly she felt right at home, right at ease, and her legs just walked her in there—right into the open bar that was closed for business. To where the band was onstage and the rehearsal was happening. Four guys were up there, dressed in shorts and tees and the lead singer had the skinny boy star look and mandatory crazy hair. She slipped in the back, enjoying the breeze from the fans, watched the drummer with envy, her fingers itching.

'I'm sorry, you can't stay here. The bar's not open yet.'

Reluctantly she dragged her gaze from the drum kit to the man who'd walked up beside her. She blinked. Once. Again. Then rapidly a couple more times to try to make her silly eyes focus. My God. So men like that really did exist? The kind that would have every woman in the vicinity immediately doing their pelvic floor exercises because they knew, absolutely knew, that keeping up with him in the bedroom would require some spectacular performance.

Sienna's whole body tensed—especially her pelvic floor.

Steely grey eyes with a smidgen of green regarded her. They were surrounded by dark lashes and topped with strongly curved dark brows. Great combination. But it was his mouth that had her flexing—the fullest, most sensual lips she'd ever seen on a man.

She blinked again and broke the contact. Looked down and in that speck of time took in his exhilarating appearance once more. He wore designer board shorts with artless ease and a close-fitting cotton tee shirt. His dark hair was clipped short and his sandals were of soft-looking leather. Details burnt into her brain in rapid-fire succession. But it was his hands she lingered on as they rested on his arms folded across his chest. Large palms and long fingers—he'd have no trouble reaching a couple of octaves on the piano. Nails so neat you'd think they'd been professionally manicured.

He must be gay.

She saw his glance slip over her as he paused too. Saw the hint of censure cloud into something else. The green light grew. The go-ahead signal. Attraction.

Not gay.

She snuck in a breath and remembered what she'd been going to ask. 'You mind if I watch a while?' Her voice seemed to have lost all power. It was some pathetic trickle of its usual timbre and the way he was looking at her, she'd lose all ability to speak or think at all. Man, he was hot.

He kept staring at her and she stared back, intrigued to see the green in his eyes intensify. His stance, with his arms banded across his chest, showed off the breadth of his shoulders and emphasised his masculine triangular shape. His shirt pulled at the seams slightly, struggling to contain the breadth of the bone and muscle beneath. Finally he opened his mouth to answer but the singer got in first.

'It's OK, Rhys. She can stay. Can you bring in the other amp?' The singer seemed to have forgotten about the microphone and shouted—the result so loud Sienna jumped. So did Mr Handsome Stranger.

Rhys. He jerked his head to the stage, looking as if he'd just remembered where he was. She saw a glance flicker between all the men, had no problem interpreting it. That was OK. She'd been in and around bands long enough to know what they thought. Groupie? Not today. Well, certainly not for any of the musicians. But Rhys their roadie? My God. She'd never seen a roadie like that before.

She watched as he walked behind the bar to wherever to get the missing equipment.

The singer smiled at her. 'Come sit and watch for a while if you want.'

She managed to work her dry mouth into some sort of smile and walked to a table near the front—one that gave a good view through to the back of the bar. She sat, stretched her legs out and let the air circulate around her, resting her body from the heat of the sun. She could cool down here for a moment and let the rhythm of the drum soothe her disgruntled soul.

Two minutes later Rhys came back in carrying a large black case. He strode past her to put it on the stage. Gave the singer a mock salute and returned to the bar. She honed in on his every movement. So much for cooling off—just looking at him made her sweat.

Across the tables, he stood level with her, looming in the corner of her eye. She tried to concentrate on the musicians but couldn't help her sidelong observance of Mr Utterly Attractive. He wasn't even trying to hide the fact he was looking at her. He stood with his back against the bar, arms across his chest again, and coolly watched her watching the band.

She forced herself to focus on the music. Succeeded for a time—well, her eyes at any rate. Her brain was still assessing his magnificent features. She caught movement to the side and no way could she not look. He'd turned to reach across the bar behind him. She watched, forgetting the musicians entirely as he stretched his body out. Under that tee was a flat wall of muscle. A perfect physical specimen. Sienna, like most people, could appreciate beauty. And his was breathtaking.

He turned back, bottle of water in his hand, and speared her gaze. With a wry turn of his lips he subtly lifted the bottle in her direction, a tiny silent toast, and then sipped.

Finding herself mirroring his swallowing action, and finding her throat rawly dry, she registered her own incredible thirst. Not necessarily for water. What it would be to lick away the drops from his lips. To have him turn into her and take her mouth, giving her exactly what she needed right now. She shivered, her heat almost a fever. She remembered herself and refocused. The slight smile, the tiny tug at the corner of his mouth put her on guard. There was knowledge in his eyes. Sinful awareness. She realised he'd had a direct view into her head and seen exactly what she'd been thinking. From his expression, he didn't think the idea was too bad either.

She turned back to the band and this time really put the blinkers on. Not going to look his way at all. Unbelievable. Her insides churned. She wanted him. He was exactly what she'd been looking for and never expected to find. A man who'd take the sexiest-man-alive title unchallenged. A man who, with just a look, told her she was beautiful.

Despondency dampened her burgeoning excitement. That look would change the minute he saw her—really saw her. Attraction would fade to pity—and fear. Sienna hated seeing fear in the eyes of a lover. It didn't exactly make her feel desirable. It didn't make her feel normal and for once, just once, she wanted normal. And that put her crazy fantasy in mind once more. Number one on her list of life experiences. She'd penned it in her journal only this morning on the beach. Front page, fifteenth volume. And she meant it this time—she was going to fulfil at least one New Year's resolution. Could she attempt it? Could she really get away with it?

She pushed a breath out as her fingers toyed with the high neck of her tee shirt. She hadn't a chance. No way could she ever manage it. Lovers tended to get naked. Sienna didn't want naked—not her at any rate—because then the fun would end and the pity party would start.

She glared at the sticks hitting the drum. Watched the relentless strike on the skin, wanting a hypnotic effect. Failed. She flicked a glance back to the bar, unable to stop her need to at least look at him one last time.

An acute and way over the top amount of disappointment flooded her when she saw he wasn't there. He'd gone.

End of fantasy.

Her thumbs itched. Hell, everything itched. She stared at the stage, the energy in her bursting to get out. She knew the sure way to make herself feel better—to beat out the blues as she had many a time. She stood and walked right up to the edge of the stage. The singer stopped and the band cut the music.

'I'm sorry. I know this is a really strange thing to ask and it's fine to say no, but would you mind if I had a turn on the drums?' Her heart raced and she looked to the drummer as she asked the final part.

'You play the drums?'

'Sure. But I'm on holiday and I haven't been near a set for a while and I'd really like to.' She flashed a smile. Hoped they wouldn't think she was some desperate groupie. Really, all she wanted was to play the drums.

'We could do with a break. Go right ahead.'

Pleasure washed through her. 'Thank you.' She took the steep step up onto the stage and headed to the back. The drummer handed her the sticks with a smile. She felt the weight of them in her hands and then set them on the snare.

She pulled her hair up off the back of her neck and twisted it into a knot on the top of her head, regretting the loss of her fifty-thousandth scrunchie. She spun the seat a few turns to lower it a little. Flexed her wrists and then rotated her hands round a couple of times. Picked up the sticks, pulled back her shoulders and sat. She tilted her head from side to side in her little pre-drumming warm-up routine. Her foot tapped and mentally she worked through the rhythm, slipping easily into the zone and feeling her body come alive. Her smile spread slow and wide across her closed mouth. *This* was exactly what she'd needed. Then she moved, hands, feet, whole body—moving separately but together to create one hell of a noise.

Rhys Maitland stood at the far end of the bar and clamped his jaw shut to stop it falling to the floor. He held his arms tight across his body as if to hold back the sudden rush of adrenalin—make that attraction. He'd been in unchartered territory since that strawberry-blonde had walked into the bar and stared right into him with those huge blue eyes of hers. His brain hadn't been working properly since. Instead he'd been filled with one thought only. Getting her naked. Yep, screaming lust central. Thing was, he had a feeling that same thing might have happened to her. She kept glancing at him, and that was definitely a good sign. Either that or he was wearing his lunch on his chin—the attention she paid to his mouth. He'd taken a sip of water to cool his internal heat, but the need to move had grown too strong and he'd slipped out the bar and back round so he could watch her from behind, so he wouldn't be sent into cardiac arrest—her eyes were more powerful weaponry than anything he'd ever encountered.

So now he stood, a picture of studied relaxation, staring at the elfin honey onstage. She looked small behind the drum kit but he knew from when he'd stood beside her that she was actually quite tall. Very slim, almost ethereal, and yet there she was thrashing the life out of those drums in a way that had him, and every other male on the premises, immobile and in awe. Her hair had been piled up on her head but as she moved it started to come down—first a couple of wisps and then the whole mass tumbled about her shoulders and down her back as she rocked on her seat in time to the beat. Heaven have mercy. Her face gently flushed with the exertion. And try as hard as he could he couldn't tear his gaze from her.

He sensed the stillness in the bar. Knew all the others were equally transfixed. Felt the flare of territorial male. She'd looked at him. And in that moment, they'd swapped something. Recognition—not of him, of his name, or who he was, but awareness of something elemental.

Like desire. Evident from the moment she'd walked in with her long, long, slim legs set off by a very cute little skirt. Her sandals were just a hint of leather straps over her feet. She was like any other babe on the beach and yet somehow totally different. She lacked the usual overtly confident quality. She'd come in, but with quiet reticence. Then her big eyes, bluer than any ocean or outback sky, had sized him up. Beneath the hesitation he'd seen a flash of bold awareness— a contradiction that had him uncharacteristically uncertain of how to progress. But, man, he wanted to progress. The unshakeable fog of ennui that had hung over him these last few weeks blown away in that one second.

Tim sidled up to him at the bar. 'Have you ever seen anything like that?'

Rhys shook his head, not trusting his voice.

'That is the hottest thing I've seen on two legs. Unbelievable.' Even Tim knew to shut up after that and enjoy the view.

After a few minutes—they could have all happily watched for hours—she stopped. Sat still on the stool for a moment, head bowed. Rhys could see her panting.

She stood and handed the sticks back to Greg, the drummer. 'Thanks, I needed that.'

'Any time.' Greg almost fell over the kit to take the sticks, his complete attention on her and not the obstacles in the way.

Tim walked up to the stage, looked up to where she stood now at the front of it. 'I'm Tim. You have to come and watch tonight. As payment, you know.'

'Sure.' She smiled and jumped down from the stage. Rhys clenched his fists even tighter at the view of her legs in action. 'I really appreciate that, guys. I feel a lot better now.'

She must have known they were all watching, tongues practically hanging out of their mouths like rabid dogs. But she walked casually as if she hadn't a care in the world, as if no one was looking, not least five full-grown, deeply red-blooded men.

She felt a lot better? Rhys' blood was pumping through his body to a far faster beat than she'd been playing on the drums. More alive than he'd been in months—yep, he felt better too. And he knew what would make him feel marvellous.

It had been so long.

He tracked her progress down the room. She was looking down and ahead of her, seemingly forgetting the band onstage behind her. Coolly ignoring the four sets of eyes trained on her back. Then she turned her head just as she passed where he was 'resting' against the bar.

Five tables stood between them as she walked down the centre aisle, but they could have been millimetres apart, such was the clarity with which he could see her eyes, almost feel their laser-like intensity. She didn't smile as she looked him over—one killer inspection. He didn't smile either, didn't move a muscle in fact—couldn't.

Unspoken communication. Unstoppable contact. That screaming lust again. Every sinew and muscle in his body tightened to the point of pain, his body wanting him to take action—to reach out and grab. At three in the afternoon with a bunch of his best mates watching?

Then she looked away and walked out of the bar. Rhys

jerked his attention back to the band. Finally remembered to breathe.

'Hot damn, that was some chick,' Tim called over to Rhys. 'Gave you the look.'

Rhys stood locked in position against the bar and managed another shrug. Yep. The look. He was still in recovery. Her eyes were haunting. Those brilliant blues had burned right through him and that message had passed again. Magnetic. Rhys was no stranger to 'the look'—the one a woman flicked a man to say she'd noticed him and was interested. That maybe he and she were a possibility.

Maybe a possibility?

She was a dead certainty. Right now he wanted her as he'd never before wanted a woman. Instant, inescapable, intense. His body was still coiled. He wanted to reach for her, wrap her around him and make her his. Restraining that urge made him ache.

Per capita Sydney had an excess of beautiful, glamorous women and Rhys was on familiar terms with several of them. But suddenly a slip of a girl in a casual tee and quick-dry skirt had nearly rendered him catatonic with need.

'The minute she finds out who you are, she's yours,' Tim said, sizing up the situation.

Rhys frowned. Wrong. She hadn't known who he was. And he didn't want her to find out. Didn't want to see that suggestion of raw physical attraction in her face replaced with attraction to something else—like dollar signs. He wanted to explore the desire without the hindrance and hang-ups that came of history and prejudice and preconceptions.

She was foreign. Had the vowel sounds of a New Zealander. Was wearing the garb of a girl who had nothing but a pack on her back. Kiwi girl on holiday. He was out of his native habitat too—in a part of the city he rarely came to.

It was almost like being in a foreign country, one where he, blessedly, wasn't known. Thus far their interaction was pretty much a blank slate. He didn't need it to be filled in. What he wanted was physical—his body sought a connection with hers and had from the second he saw her. She'd felt the pull too and he sure as hell wasn't leaving this bar again until she walked back in.

CHAPTER TWO

SIENNA dressed with more than usual care and way more than usual excitement. If ever there was a man to help her achieve number one on her list, he was that man. She'd gone back to the hostel and lain in wait for Julia and Brooke, the two South Africans she'd met on arrival last night. No sooner had she mentioned the words 'band' and 'bar' than they'd agreed to go with her. Sienna was pleased. Total party girls those two— and they'd ensure she had a good time no matter what might or might not happen with the gorgeous guy. And that was the purpose of this overseas jaunt, wasn't it? To have fun. Be normal. Seize the day.

Sienna emerged last from the bathroom, clutching her top to her. 'Can you tie these ribbons for me?'

Julia wolf-whistled. 'That is some top!'

It was. She'd only brought it with her on the spur-of-the-moment last-minute mad decision. It rolled up really small and she'd stuffed it at the bottom of her pack, never really dreaming she'd put it on. Midnight-blue satin with a matching sequin trim. The material clung from her neck to her abdomen. Three sets of long ribbons trailed. One for her neck, one for her chest and one for her stomach. Julia artfully wound them round for her. The fabric covered her from neck to belly at the front but left her back bare—other than the ribbon ties.

She twisted her head, trying to see how Julia was getting on, while ensuring the fabric was held tight to her skin. 'Quadruple knot them.'

'Are you sure? You'll need scissors to get out of it.'

'I'm sure.' That was the whole point. It was sexy and revealing but no way could anyone get underneath to discover what was below. The ribbon across her lower abdomen stopped a hand sliding up, the ribbon at the neck stopped fingers sliding south. Perfect.

She teamed it with a short black A-line skirt and high-heeled sandals. Her legs were her best feature and she intended to make the most of them. If dreams were going to come true, then she had to help them out a bit. She massaged moisturiser down the length of them. Then discreetly adjusted the strap of her underwear—a teeny, tiny lace-fronted G-string. Knickers like she never usually wore. But she was reinventing herself. And tonight she'd be as in-your-face frisky as she could get. Ribbons reached halfway down her skirt. She was covered far more than the bikini woman on the beach but was as naked as she'd ever been.

'That's a vamp outfit.' Julia stood back and surveyed her before sharply turning to her pack which had its contents spilling over the dorm floor. 'I gotta find me something to compete with that. Time to get ready and glamorise.'

As Julia's ample breasts provided more than enough competition, Sienna wasn't letting the comment go to her head. She'd never be page-three pin-up but with her legs emphasised, and her back drawing attention from her front, she might do OK.

Brooke's voice came distantly through the top she was squeezing into. 'Is the lead singer cute? You want the singer, right?'

'The singer is all yours. In fact the entire band is all yours.'

Brooke's head popped through the neck of her top. 'So who is it you're after? The bartender?'

Was it so obvious she was after someone? 'No.' She came clean. 'The band has a guy helping out.'

'You're going for the roadie?' Brooke shrieked.

'God, don't tell me he's the technical guy? Not the sound and lighting geek?'

Julia sounded appalled.

Sienna giggled. 'I'm not sure what he does. He was helping with their equipment.'

The others sent her pitying looks. 'OK, if you're sure. We'll leave him to you.'

They sat on the beds, stared into tiny compact mirrors and worked hair and make-up. Sienna twisted her hair up. Put on her mascara and gloss with a slightly heavier hand than usual and wished the hostel allowed drink in the bedrooms.

This was ridiculous. She was getting worked up—and dollied up—over nothing. He probably wouldn't even be there. She almost succumbed to the urge to cancel there and then. Time for a mental slap on the cheek. This didn't matter. She was in a foreign city, free to do as she pleased. If he was there, then she'd have a great time; if he wasn't, she'd still have a great time.

Uh-huh.

She really wanted to see him again—wanted to replay the moment she'd sizzled like a drop of water in a pan of hot oil. Just another look would be enough.

Uh-huh.

'Right, girls, let's go have ourselves a blast.' Julia gave a foxy twirl.

Sienna couldn't stop the giggles bursting out. She was such an idiot. But seeing as she was dressed to kill, she might as well go and make the most of it. She could just dance at least—as she used to with her best friend Lucy. Go and dance and have a laugh.

As they linked arms and strode down the street, Sienna soaked up some of the confidence the others oozed.

She didn't arrive until well into the second set. Rhys was at the bar, half hidden but in a place that gave him a clear view of the door—so he'd see her the minute she got there. She was with two other women. They looked like fellow tourists—tanned, relaxed, riveting. The other two were staring at the stage, she was looking around the audience. He stepped back into the shadows as her gaze swept over the bar. He wanted to observe for a while. Still deciding how or even if he would make a move. He glanced at Tim. Saw he'd seen their arrival because he winked at them. Immediately he looked straight to where Rhys stood, flashing him a huge grin.

The band wrapped up the set a song early and headed straight to her—all four of them. But it was Tim, as always, who got there first, and who less than subtly cast a glance of pure appreciation over the other two. Rhys watched for a while, wanting to see if she spent that killer look on any of the others. He saw her smile, saw her introduce her friends, but then she seemed to quieten, let the girlfriends do the talking and the flirting as they headed to the table in the back corner reserved for the band. He saw her glance around before sitting. She was looking for someone. It had better be him.

Tim came up to the bar. Ordered a tray of tequila shots, his usual *modus operandi,* then came to where Rhys stood.

'Doc, Doc, Doc. Why are you hiding out here? There's a lady at that table all wrapped up with your name on her.'

Rhys frowned. He didn't want his name out anywhere. Just for once.

'Rhys, you can't go doing the hardworking serious doctor thing all your life. You have to cut loose and have some fun some time. Hell, they've ordered you to take time off. Have a holiday, for heaven's sake. *There* is your holiday.' He jerked his head back towards the table.

Rhys managed a tight grin. They had. Made him take a fortnight. Said he was accruing too many days—a liability on the budget. They didn't want to owe him three months or more. So he'd been forced to take a break. He didn't much like breaks—they meant he had too much time to sit and think. He preferred to keep busy.

'Come on, dude. When was the last time you had a one-nighter?'

It was all right for Tim. His every action wasn't watched and subsequently detailed in the gossip pages of the local rag. If Rhys was seen within five feet of a woman it was reported the next day as a new relationship—possible wedding bells every time. The exaggeration and speculation was exhausting. The prying of paparazzi keen to rustle up a story out of nothing invaded what he'd hoped could be an ordinary existence. But Rhys knew when it came to money, especially his kind of money, people didn't scruple to sell their souls.

Mandy had done just that. Sold herself, and him, to the highest bidder. She'd taken everything he held close and hung it out for the world to see. And she hadn't even got it right. He'd asked her out on a whim. She'd been working in a café near the hospital; he'd been in there after a long shift. Her effervescence had been so attractive to his tired self. It had been a fun hour, chatting over coffee. The hour became a date, then a string of dates. He didn't figure 'til later she'd known all along who he was. That the most she understood was the wealth and status his name entailed. Too late he realised he knew nothing of the real Mandy, that nothing they had shared was real, that there was no depth beneath the bubbly exterior. He'd broken it off and then really learned how money had been her biggest motivator.

He wouldn't be fool enough to trust like that again. Not someone he didn't know. So he didn't do one-night stands. He didn't want to read all about it in the paper the next day over breakfast. Instead he did the discreet dating thing with women from his own social circle. Glamorous, beautiful for sure, but also safe, circumspect and so boring.

Tonight he could do with some anonymity—be able to have some fun and not worry about where the details might surface. He supposed he shouldn't care, should shrug it off and enjoy the reputation. But he wanted his life to be more meaningful. He refused to be the rich, spoiled playboy spending his days using his money and name to score. And he refused to be used himself.

Life, Rhys knew, was precious.

Unfortunately, that seemed to make him all the more attractive to the gutter press. And with Mandy's betrayal, telling all to anyone who'd pay enough, he'd been painted as some wounded saint—the earnest ER doctor working to escape the inanity of privileged life and the tragedy of past lessons. And that he wasn't either.

He looked back over to where the drummer girl sat at the table. Watched as she sat, smiling, her head tilted to the side as she listened to whatever it was that her friend was saying. She nodded, her smile flashing wider as she giggled. He could see the sparkle in her eyes even from this distance. Any sobering memory of Mandy's sell-out fled from his head as he focused on the stranger's golden hair and pale-skinned shoulders. His abs tightened. He sure didn't have saintly urges when it came to her. Maybe, just for once, he could do the frivolity thing. His desire for her was strong enough to tip the balance. Maybe there was a way around his issue of identity.

'She's not from here, is she?'

'Kiwi, I think. Her mates are from South Africa. Met up in the hostel they're staying at.'

Rhys stared at her some more. Felt those urges bite. Figured she was only going to be in town a night or two—what would she care if his name wasn't quite the right one? More than ever he didn't want to be himself any more. He was tired of living with his recollections and his regret. Temptation won. 'OK. I'm Rhys—she knows that, right? But she doesn't know anything else. So let's say I'm Rhys...Rhys Monroe.'

Tim stared at him, his smile slow and full of wicked disbelief. 'And what do you do for a living, Mr Monroe?'

Rhys frowned. 'Dunno. What do you think?'

'Better be something you're really crap at. The bigger the lie, the more likely they are to believe it.'

'And you know this how?'

'Rhys.' Tim looked affronted. 'I'm a professional.' He smiled at the waitress as she put the slices of lemon and dish of salt on the tray. 'Let's make you a builder.'

'A what?'

'Builder. Carpenter. You know, chippie.'

'That's ridiculous. I haven't a practical bone in my body.'

'Precisely.'

Rhys gave a grunt of laughter.

'And no way are you that Maitland guy, heir to all those millions.'

Rhys shook his head. 'Never heard of him.'

Tim picked up the tray of shot glasses. 'Well, come on, Monroe, let's get lying.'

'I'll be over in a second. Just got to finalise my persona.'

Tim winked, and, grinning broadly, headed back to the table. Rhys watched, covered by the crowd, as Tim set the tray down in front of them and handed out the shot glasses. She took one. He saw her nostrils flare as she took a sniff. Not so keen. But she did it. So did the others. Tim immediately started handing everyone a second round. She declined that one. He saw the way she pulled in her cheeks, looked over the table, glanced to the bar. Rhys smiled to himself, and summoned the waitress.

Julia and Brooke were barracking for a third shot. Sienna laughed at them. Heart sliding south as she did. Already knowing she was headed for yet another night on the sidelines. The taste of the tequila was bitterly burning her up. She couldn't handle strong alcohol, would prefer a little wine. Something light—for the lightweight she was.

No sign of the roadie. She tried to tell herself she didn't mind. Looked around the bar. Loads of men, loads. All looking good, gathering in groups. But the view was tainted. That kick of attraction had been so fierce and so foreign and she'd stupidly pinned more on it than there was. Now looking around, she couldn't help the feeling the joint was a bit of a meat market—and she didn't have the goods to set up shop.

Tim had managed to find himself a seat between the two South African beauties. Leaning back on it, talking, he soon had them laughing. The others in the band sat on chairs around them, letting Tim hold court but interjecting with witticisms of their own that had the girls shrieking even more. No doubt about it, they were a polished act and Sienna knew her place was firmly in the audience. She'd leave the participation bit to Julia and Brooke.

An arm appeared over her shoulder. 'Thought you might prefer this.' A glass was placed in front of her. Cool, clear water.

'Then you might like this.' Another glass was set alongside the first. Pale wine, just the sight of it a balm on her still-screaming taste buds.

He pulled up a chair and sat down beside her, back a little, away from the others. Dressed in black jeans and a black shirt. She could see his forearms. Lightly tanned. Muscular. Capable. He gave her a barely there grin. His face had intensity all over it—accentuated by the shadow on his jaw.

'Thank you.' She lifted the water and took a deep sip, needing it more than ever.

He watched. Before she could put the glass back on the table he took it from her. Eyes not breaking their hold, he lifted it to his sensuous, sensitive mouth and drank deeply.

'You mind sharing?' he asked belatedly.

Sienna snaked in some air. 'Not at all.'

Julia's eyebrows had disappeared under her fringe. Brooke was hammily fanning herself.

Tim dropped forward on his seat, clunking the legs down. 'Glad you could finally join us, Rhys. Let me introduce you. Julia, Brooke, this is Rhys. And I think you met Sienna earlier.'

A look passed between the two men. An even less subtle look passed between Brooke and Julia. Sienna ignored the lot of them, quickly reaching for the wine.

'Rhys is an old school friend of mine who's in town for a few days. Thought I'd get him to help us out.'

'Shouldn't you be up on that stage singing your little heart out, Tim?' Rhys interrupted.

Tim smiled a sly smile, picked up his bottle and headed back to the stage where the other band members were already strapping on instruments and quickly checking their pitch.

Julia and Brooke stared after him, then turned back and stared at Rhys, then Sienna.

'We're going to dance,' Brooke declared, grabbing Julia by the hand and leaping to her feet, eyes flashing.

'Some sound and lighting geek,' Sienna heard Julia mutter as she passed her.

'Mmm hmm.' Sienna bought some time by having another sip of wine.

Julia and Brooke hit the dance floor and headed right up the front, taking Tim's tambourine from him and starting dancing in a way that more men than just those in the band enjoyed.

Sienna watched them for a moment, loving their enthusiasm. But the strong, silent presence beside her was all she could really focus on. She turned to study him as he quietly regarded her. One thing she did know how to do was talk to people. Or, rather, how to get people to talk to her. She'd been cast in the role of confidante for so many years. The one sitting, while others achieved; she'd be the ear when they needed a rest or reviving. Ironic that she, who couldn't participate, could motivate and could listen.

'You in town for long, Rhys?'

'Just a few days. I'm a builder. From Melbourne.' He took another drink from their shared water.

OK. Keen to get the basics out. She tried to get him to elaborate a little. 'A builder?'

His attention was fixed on the band. 'Sure.'

'You don't look like a builder.'

He glanced at her then. Wry amusement in his face. 'I didn't think I'd need my tool belt tonight.'

She grinned and gave up on the small talk. He clearly wasn't one to waste words. And the most she was conscious of was her Goliath-sized awareness of him—it didn't leave much room for conversational effort.

Surprisingly he took on the task. 'What about you? What do you do?'

'Not much at the moment.'

'On holiday?'

She nodded.

'From where?'

'Life in general.' She laughed at her own pretension. Expanded so he wouldn't think she was an idiot. 'I'm in Sydney for a week before embarking on my big adventure.'

'Your OE?'

The great Overseas Experience. Obligatory for most Kiwis in their early twenties. Maybe it was something to do with being stuck in a tiny country on the edge of the earth. For a year or two or more they'd pack their packs and traipse around the world. She nodded. It had taken her a little longer to get organised, but finally she was on her way.

'Europe?'

'South America initially.' There were a couple of things on her life's must-do list that she wanted to finally cross off. Peru was right up there.

'So where is home?'

She shrugged. 'I'm not sure yet.' It wasn't where she'd come from. She loved it. She loved the people but she needed space to set her life in its new direction. 'What about you?'

'I've a couple of weeks off. Just spending it hanging out in Sydney.'

'Catching up with old friends?'

'Right now I'm more interested in making new ones.'

Silence fell again. His eyes held hers as he took another sip—this time of her wine. She wished he wouldn't. She really did because all she then saw was that beautiful mouth with its perfect cupid bow. Since when did she feel jealous of a glass? But how would it feel to be pressed against his lips, to have his tongue lick her rim?

She felt heat rise in her cheeks. The way she was thinking! And the worst of it was she was certain he knew. Possibly even thinking the same. Because his attention was fixed on her when she took the glass from him and sipped.

He waited until she'd placed her glass back on the table

before leaning closer to her, speaking with the world's most tempting voice.

'You know what I think, Sienna?'

'What?'

'I think you should dance with me.'

A flicker of excitement ran from the nape of her neck all the way down her spine, through her legs and to her toes. She wriggled them in her sandals. 'OK.'

They stood. Julia and Brooke were somewhere up the front, playing up to Tim's 'glam lead singer' act. Sienna stopped in the middle of the crowd, wanting to disappear into it. Not wanting to feel any more self-conscious than she already was. Fully aware that Tim and the other band members were probably watching. That Brooke and Julia would be giving the thumbs-up behind Rhys' back. She didn't want the distraction or the discomfort.

Within three seconds she wouldn't have cared if there were a film crew beside her broadcasting the action live to twenty million viewers. She'd totally lost awareness of all others, of their surroundings. She lost all sense of everything except Rhys. The thrill rippled through her—her awareness of him almost a tangible entity. They took advantage of the crowd on the floor to stand close. He smiled and she found herself smiling back, just like that. So easy. The music wasn't too heavy, he moved, she followed. Fingers brushed. She nearly jumped, the electricity practically sparking. She glanced at her hand. Quickly looked to gauge his reaction—had he felt that current? He was watching her face, then looked to her hand. With slow deliberation he reached out and took it in his, his grip firming at her tremble.

If she felt this on edge with just one small touch, how on earth would anything more feel? All she knew was that she wanted that more—with a biting need, almost desperation. Desire both ferocious and foreign.

Neither of them was smiling any more. They moved closer as the floor became more crowded. He didn't take his eyes off her. Shadows fought with emerald light. His hold on her hand tightened.

'I know this is really forward. And I know I don't really know you. And feel free to say no, but...'

'But what?'

He looked straight into her eyes with a wry turn-up of his mouth. 'I'm going to kiss you.'

Sienna stopped moving. Stood stock-still in the middle of the dance floor while a hundred others grooved close around her. Her initial reaction was relief—that she hadn't been dreaming, that the attraction wasn't all one-sided. The relief soon gave way to electric excitement. She provoked it further, confidence surging through her. 'Well, that's good, because I intend to kiss you right back.'

He'd stopped dancing too. Abandoned the pretence of caring about the music. Green eyes, not slate, burned into her. 'That's good.'

He stepped nearer. Her body screamed for the touch of his. But it was still out of range—the millimetres feeling like miles. Yet there was almost reluctance between them. A tacit agreement to draw it out, to savour the moment that they'd both been seeking since first seeing each other. She sensed it in him, the deliberate decision to take time to truly appreciate each moment.

Anticipation immobilised her. As much as she wanted to move, it was he who would have to take that final step.

He did. His hand came up, traced her cheek and jaw with a light finger. She quelled the tremor inside. Her lips were tingling. She just had to lick them, had to.

'No,' he muttered. 'Let me.'

He bent to her. Very gently touched the tip of his tongue to the full centre of her lower lip.

Sensation engulfed her. This was crazy. But the fire ripping through her was real.

His hands, gentle, went to frame her chin.

'Better?'

'No.' She tried to hide the shaking, not wanting to admit to the extremity of her reaction.

'Still thirsty?'

Desperately so. She managed a minute nod. Her chin tilted up to meet him, her neck arched to its full length.

His hand slid around it so his fingers tangled into her hair at the back. How she wanted that mouth—that beautiful mouth...

He touched her again. Brushed his lips over hers a couple of times. Such soft teasing that tore at her self-control. She reached up and mirrored his action, threading her fingers into the thick hair at the back of his head, pulling him down to her.

They stood completely still in the mass of movement. Unable even to sway in time, concentrating wholly on each other, on the fragile softness that would shatter if their passion was unleashed. This wasn't the place for it to be unleashed. Yet she knew it was impossible to hold back.

A moment of fantasy melded with reality. Just this once.

He lowered his head as she lifted her chin. They met at the middle, lips catching and clinging. Mouths opening so tongues could taste—deep and delicious.

He kissed his way down the length of her neck, and back up to her ear. 'You are quite the most beautiful thing.' He pulled back to look at her, his gaze heavy and gleaming.

She ensured her lips curved upwards but dropped her lashes so he wouldn't see the pain she knew her eyes would have reflected. Beautiful? Not entirely.

She tugged on his hair, directing him back to her mouth. Wanting the words to end and only the feeling to remain. Not wanting compliments or pretty phrases or promises to falsely gild this moment. Because that was all it was—one moment, but one of absolute bliss. The kind of moment she'd wanted all her adult life and one she wanted to extend. She wanted to make the most of the magic in the night. She melted into him in a way she'd never do at home. But she wasn't at home. She wasn't with anyone she knew.

The sexiest man she'd ever laid eyes on was holding her and kissing her as if she was the sexiest thing *he'd* ever seen. There was no one who knew to tell him otherwise. She'd keep up this pretence as long as she possibly could.

Their bodies collided as passion rose. Initial restraint fast fading as they recognised their needs matched.

More.

At the first touch of his fingers on her bare back, her body shook—the electric charge bolting through her system again. He jerked his head back, his startled green eyes reading hers. She registered the same aftershock in them. He opened his mouth to speak but she stretched forward, reaching right up on tiptoe to prevent him. Not wanting to name it, just wanting to experience it.

Again.

His fingers traversed, burning fire as they went. The need to have them touch her all over nearly crippled her. Instead she spread fingers and palms across his shoulders. Wanting to experience the feel of him as much as the way he made her feel.

So this was what Cinderella must have felt like. To have met her Prince Charming, to be dancing, but knowing it was a fantasy that couldn't last past the midnight hour.

Make the most of it.

Time constraint made her bolder. She basked in his openly hungry gaze. He wanted her and she wanted nothing but that mouth roving over every inch of her.

No. Not every inch. She forced the miserable thought back, stepped closer into his embrace. Determined to take what she wanted while she could. And he met her, sensed her availability without censure, simply giving her what she asked for and more.

She'd never been so forward in all her life. And she loved it. It wasn't really the kind of kiss that should be in public at all. She was locked in his arms, length to length they pressed together hard. Both feeling the desperate need to seep into each other's bodies. To somehow transcend the clothing, the fabric between them and to merge into one.

What had begun as a slow, sensuous dance flavoured with restraint had now become frankly hot and heavy and not nearly enough. His hands traced over her back, fingers that had fluttered over her soft skin now stroked with increasing insistence. His palms pressed her towards him—closer but still not as close as she wanted. She ached, a real physical pain deep inside that only he could soothe—by being deep inside her.

His hand came to rest on her bottom, curved over it with pressure, pulling her tight into him. Locking them pelvis to pelvis. The feel of his erection against her was the most exquisite torture. Half of her trembled, the other half imbued with a surge of strength that had her moving in a way to torment him too. Hunting out the response her basic instinct demanded she receive—him driven to take.

His grip grew stronger, his kisses more frantic—trailing across her face, down her neck. Her eyes closed. Her breath came short and fast—faster and faster until she was panting, almost pleading.

His jaw brushed rough against her over-sensitised skin as he raised his head with sudden and unexpected force. 'We shouldn't be here any more.' His voice was low and husky and his hands tightened, keeping her close. 'I think we need to be alone.'

Green eyes searched hers. She knew they were seeking out doubt. But she had no intention of stepping away. For the first time in her life she ignored her worry and just went with the want.

'Somewhere close.' Miraculously her voice worked.

'You're sure?'

Again the intensity together with a sensitivity she hadn't expected. And faint hesitancy just as there had been when they had first hit the dance floor. Desire most certainly, but something else as well. Some other thought, small but inescapable, that had him pausing. But as he pulled on her arm it seemed that he, like she, had no choice.

She gave him the only possible answer. 'As sure as you are.'

CHAPTER THREE

THE door closed behind them, muting the noise of bottles, beat and bar. Sienna was in some oversized pantry. Half-dazed, she took in the shelves where giant jars of sun-dried tomatoes vied for space next to sacks of rice and tins of whatever. Rhys had taken her by the hand and led her off the dance floor. Known exactly where he was headed. She'd simply followed, unquestioning. He closed the door behind him. Bolted it. Swung her so her back was to the door, the lock just by her arm. He nodded to it.

'You can leave any time.'

'I don't want to.'

She saw his tension as he braced against the door but holding his body away from her. She looked along the length of his arms, pinning her in. She could see the strength in them. Not overdeveloped, bulging biceps, but defined, long muscles that were, frankly, beautiful. She sensed he was pushing against the door as a way to keep himself in check. She didn't want him to hold back. No restraint, she wanted everything. Wanted him to want her in the deeply physical way she wanted him, and she wanted to feel it, experience it. All.

It was her turn to seize the moment. Daring, she reached

out quickly before habit returned and she hesitated. She unfastened the top button of his shirt. She heard the catch of his breath. A tiny smile tugged the corners of her mouth. This could be an awful lot of fun. And she'd gone too long without fun. Well, not tonight.

Her fingers shook only a little as she worked the buttons with surprising ease. Until both halves of the shirt hung apart and she was able to see his taut bronzed torso. The initial attack of butterflies in her tummy was fast replaced by a serious tightening. Transverse, internal and external obliques—all those abdominal muscles tensed at the sight of raw male in perfect prime.

She must have a fairy godmother to grant her this wish. She forced her gaze from his torso to his face. She could see the way he'd clamped his jaw shut as he watched her admiring him.

Their eyes met. She saw the serious look in his again. The reality of what she was considering hit her.

She spoke. 'I don't usually…'

'Neither do I.'

Somehow she knew that was true. 'I just want to…'

'Me too.'

Touch.

She reached a hand out sideways and flipped the light switch. Blackness covered them—sudden and total. She couldn't even make out his outline. But she could hear him. Could sense his nearness.

'Sienna?'

'Indulge me.' She smiled—excited by his audible tension, amused by her actions. She even sounded like a seductress. She slipped her panties down, kicking them off and to the floor. Now she felt like one. A sense of exhilaration flooded her. Freedom. In the dark, where there was only touch and scent and sensation, she could be as wicked and wild as she wanted.

'How should I indulge you?' The tension was still there, and a trace of husky desire.

'Touch me.'

He stepped closer. She heard the movement of his feet. With the loss of vision her other senses seemed more acute.

His voice lowered but she still heard every word as clear as the beat of the drum. 'Where should I touch you?'

'Anywhere you want.' Everywhere. She didn't mind. In the dark like this, anything could happen.

He was close. Very close but still not touching and she wanted that beyond belief.

She smelt the wine they'd drunk. Then caught a hint of a scent new to her but thoroughly delightful—Rhys. Aroused.

But still he held back.

Her breasts ached. She longed to feel him caress them—to both soothe and set on fire. As for his mouth, the kind of luscious lips that overly wealthy housewives paid thousands for. The perfect Cupid's bow. She wanted that *everywhere*. Where was he? Panic gripped her—he hadn't changed his mind?

Then he spoke, that low sound of temptation personified. 'I can't quite decide where to touch and whether to use my hands or mouth.'

'How about both? Everywhere.'

She heard his puff of amusement and his low murmur. 'Sienna the Siren.'

At last he touched her, his hands settling on her waist as his lips sought hers. Back to the beginning—but it wasn't a beginner's kind of kiss. Deeper, long, lush kisses followed— lasting for ever. His hands moved, played up her back, and then slipped round her front, his fingers seeking her softness. The ache in her breasts intensified, wanting more.

He spoke her desire aloud. 'I want to touch you. How do I get this off?' He tugged at the material.

'It's complicated. I…'

His groan sounded half smothered. 'Later, we'll get rid of it later.'

Regret whistled through her. There would be no later. But the thought was wiped from her mind as his hands encircled her braless breasts, and his mouth found her nipple with killer precision.

Raw need ricocheted through her. She felt the pull in every limb. Her brain forcing her entire body to attend to the sensation in her nipples. Never had she felt so desired. Never had her breasts received such attention. Such deliberate and devastating touches. Lovers were usually distracted by then—by the scar. Tonight, despite the thin, slippery fabric covering her, she could feel his desire, the wet heat of his mouth as he caressed her with a physical want she knew would wane if he ever saw her in entirety.

She rocked her pelvis against him—an unconscious desire to soothe the ache that had sprung there. Then she realised her body, her very sex, was demanding the same kind of attention her breasts were receiving. The essence of her wanted his fingers, his lips, his tongue to delve and devour the way they were her rounded flesh.

She wanted everything he had. All of his body. All of his strength.

The scent of the room, the sound of her, the softness of her skin and the heady darkness all combined to give Rhys the feeling he'd left this earth and entered some sort of heaven. He ran his hands over her breasts and back, partly wanting to pull her into him, partly wanting her on a pedestal so he could worship each delicious bit of her.

He was spinning so far out of control. He needed to step back. Regroup a little. Hell, he couldn't even remember if he had a condom in his wallet. Did he have one? Think, brain. *Think.* But she was kissing him again and rational thought was becoming impossible. In this darkness, the cool room wasn't that cool at all. Her long hair tickled his skin and he found himself weaving his hands into it again and again. Running fingers through its silky softness as she kissed his chest, her hands firmly smoothing down his abs. And suddenly he could see it—there was nothing in his mind but the bright, burning gold. Flaxen flames. A gorgeous mess that was so striking and so seductive. He pulled her close for another deep kiss, couldn't keep away any longer, wanting to touch her most intimate space. From the way her hips writhed against his he knew she wasn't about to say no.

He bent his knees so he could place a palm on each leg, halfway up her thighs. He heard her breathing hitch. He kissed her softly, kept close so he could catch every nuance of her reaction as he slowly slid his hands towards home. Her legs were slim but he could feel their supple strength. As he traced up towards where they gently curved together he saw them in his mind's eye—a heaven-sent pillow. After this, when they were in his bed, he would rest his head there and explore the treasure at the top—at length. Right now, his fingers were sending him the images, his ears supplying the audio. Her shallow snatches of air accelerated as he neared his destination. Little gulps turned into little groans and he was seized by the desire to hear her sounds as she came. He'd make sure that happened very, very soon.

He reached the curve of her bottom, the cleft of her sex. And his pleasure in assessing her reaction was totally toppled by the realisation she wasn't wearing any underwear. He had complete access. His mind blanked. But his body knew what to do—make use of it. He traced through her wet warmth, and the scent of her secret space slipped out, filling him, tempting him. He had to taste her. He had to take her. He'd plunge deep into this woman, no matter what.

He was so busy concentrating, so busy deciding, he didn't really register she'd been fiddling at his waist, not until he felt his belt pulled away. How she got his zip down he didn't know but it was blessed relief as his erection sprang free from the denim prison.

With surprising strength she placed one hand on the back of his head, pulling him into a kiss while the other grasped his straining penis. Her hand was warm and firm and she was stroking him and he choked a growl into her mouth. He needed to pull back for a moment or it would be all over in a few more seconds.

And then she jumped. Literally jumped into his arms. Instantly, instinctively, he moved, righting his balance, spreading his legs wide so he could bear both his weight and hers. He had no choice but to have his hands under her bottom, supporting her as she wrapped around him.

God, it felt good. He felt her wetness right on him. Agonisingly close. Then she shifted. He heard the little noise—a cross between a sigh and a cry—as she wriggled and slid onto him. Right down, naturally adjusting her angle so she took him in to the hilt. Her legs locked around him.

Oh, yes!

Sudden. Shocking. And so incredibly satisfying he almost came right away.

Not yet! Not yet! Not yet!

Sucking in air, he fought it. Holding back with an effort sure to shave a few years off his life. His heart thundered. She was so hot, so wet and so wanting. But he couldn't think about it, couldn't indulge immediately. His breath calmed as control returned to him—although he knew it wouldn't be for long.

'You OK?'

Hell, he'd wanted to ensure she was really ready for him, had half planned not to do this until they were in a bed rather than some tiny cupboard at the back of a bar.

But there was no way he could stop now and here she was the one asking if he was coping all right.

'Too fast?'

'A little.' Answering honestly, he pushed out some air. 'But I've got you now.'

He sure did. Hot and sweet. He kissed every inch of her he could reach, squeezed her sweet rounded bottom as he supported her. He wanted this to go a little slower but she was riding him, pressing him home to victory in a way he couldn't resist for much longer. He groaned. Reminded himself this was just the appetiser. The prelude to a fantastic evening ahead where they would lie and roll in a bed over and over, again and again. A room where he would rip the clothing from her if he had to so he could see her as well as feel her, hear her without the backdrop of noise from an overcrowded bar in full party mode. And with that thought relieving him he gave in to the desire to simply take what she was offering. To plunge in deeper and harder and hold her so he could claim her with all his strength.

Her legs curled tighter around him, vice-like she gripped him. Her whimpers of delight turned into cries of celebration as her tension snapped. He felt the waves washing over her, radiating out to him, threatening to swamp him.

And incredibly he didn't explode. Instead he found himself in a new phase, even more intense, where he had even more energy, strength to keep holding her, supporting her while she contracted around him again and again. He pushed inside, further and further, the heated silk of her body absorbing him, the strokes of pleasure almost sending him out of his mind.

More, more, more!

She was coiling tighter again, uttering soft, broken murmurs that sounded like screams to him, they pierced him so intensely. He wanted them louder, wanted her harder.

He growled as he adjusted his stance, tightening his fingers on her, no longer able to keep from bruising, just needing with a kind of possessive and primal instinct that was as foreign to him as it was raw.

He switched his hold, freeing one hand so he could grasp her by her hair, pulling her mouth to his, taking it in a kiss that was hard and hungry and utterly unrestrained.

She gave as good as she got. Her tongue came out—eagerly searching, tasting deep into him, and as he released her from the kiss she came after him, her tongue seeking his lips, tracing their curve and then nipping at them. Her fingers curled into his hair, tugging, holding him so he couldn't escape the heat of her kiss. She took all his breath and demanded more. She was devouring him—raw, relentlessly seeking and giving pure physical pleasure.

And he could fight it no longer. Gave her what she sought. A male body, aroused beyond control, possessively thrusting, pulsating with pleasure, pouring in everything he had until he was utterly, utterly spent.

The bright, burning gold light exploded in his head.

And then there was blackness.

Her weight was no longer his sweet burden. Her legs were gone from his waist. His hands hung, unusually useless, as he tried and failed to get his body working again. He whistled air into his burning lungs—rough and ragged.

He felt her fingers on his neck as she pulled his head down to hers. He felt her warm breath in his ear. He heard the jerky whisper.

'Thank you.'

Before he could reply, she'd slid back the bolt and opened the door, escaping into the passage between bar and restaurant and pulling it shut again quickly behind her.

Rhys blinked. Colour spots floated in front of him, caused by the split second of harsh light. Plunged into blackness again, he reached forward. Palms hit wood.

Hell. She was gone.

He braced his hands on the door, light-headed from the expenditure of energy and sheer disbelief over the intensity of the moment he'd just experienced. Blood rushed all over. To his body, not his brain. That he couldn't seem to work. He couldn't seem to move at all. Stunned. Sapped of all strength.

Then he felt the sweat running off his brow. Felt the way his shirt was sticking to his back. Felt the burn in his thighs and arms, his muscles now seizing from the effort of taking her weight, taking her completely for he didn't know how long.

He pressed the light on his watch. Hell. They'd been in here over an hour. Had she turned him into some tantric sexpert? Rhys was no stranger to a sustained sex session, but he'd never managed quite such a marathon before. And the thing was it wasn't enough. He wanted more. Incredibly he wanted more this minute. He straightened. His body recharged in only those few milliseconds and filled with the need to seek and conquer. Again. Now.

He found the light switch, fastened his jeans, and stuffed a couple of shirt buttons through holes. He gave a quick glance round the cold store—amazingly not a thing appeared out of place. In the small square foot of space in the centre of the room the earth had shifted, reality had receded, and yet not one grain of rice had hit the floor. For a second he frowned—had he just imagined that whole thing? Maybe the hospital had been right and he really, really needed this holiday. Was his brain reduced to feeding him the ultimate fantasy? Losing it, definitely losing it.

Then he caught sight of the slip of black. He bent and retrieved it. A faint, tantalising scent whispered to him. It registered and hit hard in the groin. Her panties. She must have slid them off right at the start. He smiled at their size—a scrap of lace and nothing. He paused, thinking the encounter through. She'd known exactly what she wanted from the start. His smile faded, frown returned. What had gone on tonight? Had she had a hidden agenda? But she'd seemed so genuine. She'd seemed as blown away as he had. Doubt rushed in with anger hot on its heels as an evil thought occurred to him. Maybe she did know who he was. Maybe she'd known his identity exactly and targeted him. And he'd been the fool. Had he just fallen prey to the biggest honey trap ever? And was a million-dollar baby her prize? The Mandy mess would be nothing compared to that.

His blood pumped faster. He knew nothing about her. And he'd just had unprotected sex with her. Stupid. Reckless. Risky. Rhys didn't do risk. He always ensured he retained control of a situation—never allowing circumstance to change so vulnerability could be possible. Vulnerability led to disaster. That he did know.

But he hadn't been in control of that situation—she had. She'd sprung on him, surprised him and—got what she wanted? For once he'd just let go, gone with something that had felt so incredibly good he hadn't had the strength to fight it. Been tempted by the whole holiday idea, the fun of forgetting who he was for a while. Was he now going to pay the price?

Seriously angry with himself, he yanked his belt. Angry with Tim for bringing him to this hellish haven for traveller types. Hell, he couldn't even blame booze for that moment of madness. It had been all-consuming lust. He'd been unable to think beyond having her, hearing her, being in her.

Again. He still wanted it.

Jaw clamped, he stuffed the delicate garment into his jeans pocket. He'd better find her damn fast. And find out exactly what kind of game she was playing. He burst out of the pantry—ignored the startled yelp of the bartender who, with unfortunate timing, happened to be walking past the door.

Rhys strode into the bar. Only a few seconds had passed but that could be her make-or-break advantage. And she had wanted to escape. But the bar was thick and crowded. Thankful for his superior height, he soon spotted the divine stretch of skin that was her back as she slowly threaded her way through. She was almost at the door. He barrelled through the masses, uncaring of knocking someone, hearing the glass fall. He muttered an unintelligible apology that wouldn't have been heard anyway, given he was already three paces past. His eyes were glued to the prize. But then she was out the door. Left. She turned left.

He reached the exit and whipped his head to spot her. There. Several yards along. Even from the distance he could see she was struggling. Her hand rose to her head, fingers knotted in her hair to hold it back from her face. She seemed oblivious to the storm that threw wind and rain at her.

Humidity's hold had been shattered, but until now Rhys hadn't noticed either. The sound of thunder had been disguised, not by the beat of the band, but by the cacophony of their sighs and whispers in the cold store. Her song still rang in his ears, driving him to follow her. Fast. The large drops of rain pelting him were a relief, cooling his lust and anger-heated body.

Something stopped him from calling out to her. He wanted

to see where she was going first. Hoped like hell she wasn't about to disappear into a taxi—he could see the lights of one at the stand not too far ahead. Only the one vehicle. Damn.

But instead she turned, stepping through the brightly lit doorway. He read the sign in a second. A hostel. Backpacker paradise. So maybe one part of her story checked out. On the surface at least she was on holiday.

He entered in time to see her ankles disappearing up the stairs. He went to follow but the guy on Reception nobbled him.

'Can I help you?'

'The woman who just went past here. Slim, strawberry-blonde.'

The doorman blinked lazily.

'She's staying here?' Rhys rapped out the question.

'I can't give out information about our customers.'

'So she is staying?'

The bland expression remained.

'More than one night?'

No answer again, but there was a suspicion of a wink.

Rhys savoured the slight satisfaction but it wasn't enough. He'd get all the answers, thank you very much. Utter irritation, unquenchable desire, undeniable need to know forced his actions. 'Got any vacancies?'

'Dormitory or own room?'

He thought for a moment—wicked intent winning over cold curiosity. 'Got any doubles?'

The door guy grinned. 'Sure.' He pulled a form and started filling it in. 'I need name and details, how many nights you want and I need ID—passport or driver's licence.'

Damn. He didn't want to reveal who he was. 'Can't I just pay up front? Cash?'

'We still need ID.'

Rhys deliberated for a nanosecond. Privacy was precious—but the guy on the desk was an American. He'd have no idea who he was. He'd be in the clear. Just one night—so he could find her over breakfast and ask what the hell was going on. So he handed over his driving licence. Filled in the forms. Got the key.

He finally got to go up the stairs she'd ascended ahead of him. He unlocked his room. He even had his own mini-bathroom. Not bad for a cheap-as-they-come hostel. Although he was paying the 'premium' rate for his own room and *en suite*. He wondered where she was right now. Under this roof—but in a room full of bunks or on her own? Was she thinking of him?

Hell—was she with someone else?

He rejected that idea immediately. There had been hesitation—he was sure he'd seen that in the blue sea of her eyes. She had said she didn't usually...

What? Go for millionaire heirs? It wouldn't be the first time some stunner had used him to bag herself a fortune. Different style from Mandy, same result. Money. Only this would be even more damaging. He'd be left with a permanent reminder of his folly—no child deserved to be brought into being purely to serve as a bargaining chip, a commodity. He had to find her and fix this.

He swore. How had he managed to lose control so entirely? Irritated, he stood for as long as he could under piping hot water. Sluicing the sweat from his body, he also rinsed his shirt while he was at it, hanging it up where it would dry quick-time. The storm had abated, the temperature would only rise again.

He thought about her parting words. *Thank you.* Simple. Strangely heartfelt. He hardened his own heart. He was not going to be suckered by a burning blonde. Just because she had a nice hint of vulnerability in her eyes that threatened to soften even his roughened-up skin.

But in the steam of the room, memories of their dark encounter flew at him, tormenting him. He turned the tap to cold, glanced at his watch and groaned. It was going to be a long few hours. But no way was she getting away with whatever the hell she had planned.

Although what he was going to do about it, he had no idea.

CHAPTER FOUR

SIENNA sat on the sand and watched the sun rise. The dawn
of a new day, and a different Sienna. She chuckled at her
dramatic moment. But she felt changed. And she would
always thank him for it. She'd escaped the dorm as early as
she could, not wanting any kind of post-mortem with Julia
and Brooke. Last night was not for analysing. She'd feigned
sleep when they'd stumbled back in at stupid o'clock. Really
she'd lain awake almost all the remainder of the night.

She stretched out on the sand, rotating her ankles in circles.
Half tempted to ease the slight stiffness with some exercises,
but mostly tempted not to. Deciding to keep the gentle aches
as a reminder of the most physical and intense experience of
her life. Her body still felt warm and pliant from the contact
with his. Still felt wet and wanting.

She'd never had a one-night stand before and she refused
to regret it. She only regretted that it couldn't be more. She
grabbed her day pack. Sipped from her water bottle and pulled
out her new journal. She never went anywhere without it.
She'd kept one for years—had volumes locked away in a
suitcase in the attic of her mother's house. It wasn't so much
a 'today I did x, y and z' kind of diary, but a personal place
to explore her dreams and fears. For years it had been largely

fears. She'd recognised early on that she couldn't talk to her mother, brother or even her best friend about those fears because doing so upset them. They worried about her enough. So she developed the skill to listen to others, talk but keep her own anxieties to herself.

Writing was her way of making sense of what was happening in her life. But despite the weightiness of past events, for the first time she felt unable to pen a word, let alone a sentence. She stared unseeing across the sea, flashes of the previous night filling her mind. Impossible. She could never capture that beauty in words. Unable to record what had happened, let alone how she felt about it.

She looked back down to her book, with a thinly protected heart read over the list of her life's must-dos. The list she always wrote at the start of each year in the front of the new journal. Always hoping to cross at least one or two off in the course of the year. As the years had progressed the list had grown longer not shorter, more fanciful, humorous, outrageous.

But she'd done it. Number One could be crossed off. The one that had made her simultaneously blush and giggle as she'd written it. A joke. A fantasy. And it had been more fantastic than she'd ever imagined. Hell, she'd never imagined it could actually be a reality. Despondent, she recapped her pen. To record it would diminish it and it had been so profound, so perfect. She stared again at the water, watching the sun sparkle on the rippling waves. She wished she weren't such a girl over this. Wished the niggle of guilt would leave her.

She had no idea how long she'd been sitting there, but she wasn't alone any more. There were people arriving with sunscreen and shades. She should get up and get some breakfast. Face the world again. But she didn't move—couldn't be bothered and she sure wasn't hungry.

She played with the sand, drawing up a handful and letting

it run through her fingers. She'd feel better soon. She had so much to look forward to—this was merely a wait in the wings before her adventure. But she wished for more of last night's adventure—more of him. She felt bad for not explaining things to him. He'd been wonderful and she'd just disappeared. It wasn't her usual style. None of it had been her usual style—and that had been the whole point. To have been able to have it like that she'd had to leave.

She'd struggled to find her way out of the bar at first. Disoriented. Dazed. The crowd had seemed crazy. She'd forgotten other people existed. She'd felt so cocooned in that darkness. She hadn't wanted to go. Her body had ached to lie with his, to sleep curled beside his. It had hated the fact she was walking away. It had not been what was meant to happen. They had been supposed to rest. And then do it all again.

She shook off the sand, picked up the pen again, pulling the cap off and replacing it, over and over.

'Did you sleep well?'

She jerked her head up, dropping the pen and her jaw as she looked at the tall person towering over her.

Oh, God, it was him.

'What—you didn't expect to see me again?'

She snapped her journal shut, and her mouth. Stuffed the fabric-covered, hardbound book into the bottom of her bag. Bought some more time by hunting for the lid of the pen, but it was lost for ever in the sand. Hot blood burned in her cheeks. 'Um. I…um…'

'I didn't sleep too well, actually, thanks for asking.'

She cleared her throat, but still couldn't get words to come out.

'You see, I met this girl—'

'Rhys,' she croaked.

'Oh. You remember my name.'

'Of course I remember your name!'

He squatted down beside her. And she saw into his face properly. Got a shock. He was looking ferocious. Angry as hell.

She got in quickly then, words flying. 'Look, I'm really sorry about last night.'

'I'm not. Yet. I hope I'm not going to be.'

Confusion deepened the burn in her face.

His eyes, mainly slate, captured hers. 'Like, in nine months time going to be sorry. The mother of all honey traps, was it?'

'What?' Her clammy hands covered her inferno-like flush. She grasped his implication. Nine months? As in B-A-B-Y? He thought she used him to get pregnant? As if.

'Contraception is covered, trust me.' She choked the words out. Marriage and children might be on most people's list of life ambitions but they'd never be on hers. She didn't want any child of hers living the kind of cloistered life she'd suffered and she didn't want to commit to someone only to have to leave them too soon—as her father had left her mother.

The hardness in his eyes didn't soften a jot. 'It's a dangerous game you play.'

'I don't. I...I really don't do that,' she stammered. Annoyed with her mortification. Annoyed that she felt the desperate need to defend herself against his thoughts. It shouldn't matter. But it did. He'd been amazing. And she'd just snuck off. She wanted to slink away now. But couldn't. He thought she was some hideous tramp?

'I meant it when I said I didn't usually...' She faltered under his implacability, finally looking away. 'I'm so embarrassed. I got carried away. It was the tequila slammers.'

'You only had one.'

'I had more before you arrived.'

'Rubbish. I was watching you from the moment you walked in.'

She swallowed. Nerves stretching taut—how could she possibly explain this to him?

'You spend all your holidays having one-nighters with people you hardly know?' He laughed. It sounded dangerously like a snarl. 'It wasn't even one whole night, just a turgid hour. A quick lay and you're off. Did you find someone else for the rest of the night?'

'No!' Anger settled in her. She would not have him demean their experience. OK, so she hadn't been particularly thoughtful, but there was no need for things to turn nasty. 'No. That's sleazy. What we did was not sleazy.'

'What was it, then?'

'A beautiful memory.'

He paused at that. When he spoke again it was softer. 'Past tense?'

She looked back to the sea, not wanting to see him and suffer the bitter temptation of something she couldn't ever have again. 'Past.'

There was a long silence. She hoped he'd take the hint and leave. Her heart was fraying round the edges. Was this why so many women regretted one-night stands? There really was no such thing as 'just walk away'. Things always got complicated.

She wasn't naïve enough to think you could fall in love with someone after a one-night stand. But she certainly cared about what he thought. Too much. It was only because he'd done something for her that no one else ever had been able to. The stars had been aligned, maybe there had been a full moon—some sort of mysterious magic? Anyhow, it was a one-off—those circumstances couldn't be repeated.

He didn't leave, rather he sat on the sand, stretched his legs out alongside hers.

He still had the same shirt on but it was looking rumpled. His tanned arms were tense. More stubbly shadow darkened his jaw. The cold light of day—and he was even more gorgeous. Wilder looking than last night, but that, she suspected, was because he was feeling a little wild. With her.

Fair enough.

She felt compelled to talk honestly. 'I didn't expect to see you again.'

He lay back, resting on his elbow, the length of his beautiful body shown off. Hers went all soft inside and she overcompensated—tensing on the outer.

'You just ran into the night like Cinderella, only you didn't leave me a glass slipper, you left me these.'

Mortified, she watched as he pulled her panties out of his pocket. A scrap of lace and elastic. Looking a lot like something a streetwalker would wear.

It was an effort to speak—a squeak, really. 'Can I have them back?'

'No.' A half-smile quirked the corners of his mouth up. 'I don't think you can. Because, unlike you, for me that hour wasn't anywhere near enough.'

'I'm sorry?'

'Last night was an appetiser. My appetite is well and truly whetted. I want you in a bed, my bed, with all the hours of darkness ahead of us.'

Colour flooded her. Top to toe. She knew it did. She could hear blood beating in her ears, feel it in her cheeks, the palms of her hands. Even her ankles were blushing—her knees. Actually blushing. And it wasn't just embarrassment.

It was the most words he'd strung together in the short time she'd known him and she wished he hadn't because his voice was rich and deep and she couldn't help but listen—and be seduced. And she couldn't help but look at his mouth as it moved and really those lips alone were seductive enough.

As for what he'd actually said...

The blush deepened. But she didn't have a chance in succeeding a second time. She'd have to get naked—and that she didn't want to do. She'd never forgotten the look on Neil's face. The way he'd recoiled. *Everything* would change.

'One night. What do you say? Finish off what we started.'

She melted more into the sand.

'It was only the beginning, you know.'

If she had any kind of backbone she'd stand and walk away. But her bones weren't there any more, there was just mush. Wanting, so badly, what she couldn't have.

He sat up. 'Tell you what, I think we've done this all round the wrong way—topsy-turvy. Back to front. Did the sex before the date. Let's do the date now.'

'I'm sorry?'

'I'm serious. Dinner, a drink, some conversation. I think you owe me that at least.'

It was so tempting. And she did owe him. Could she even manage telling him the truth? No. She didn't want to, didn't want to see desire fade. She wanted to maintain the memory. Maybe, if she was careful, she could add to it just a teeny bit.

Rhys watched the conflict cross her face. She wanted to, but didn't want to. Sitting there blushing like a schoolgirl. Apparently mortified over her wildness the previous night. Not her usual behaviour—that was for sure. You couldn't fake a bodily reaction like that blush. Just as you couldn't fake the fire between them.

He felt happier than the moment he learned he'd come first in his final med exams. Initial instinct had been right. It wasn't a ruse. She had no idea who he was. She wasn't out for a million-dollar baby. He believed her about the contraception. She'd wanted him. Still wanted him. So why the up-and-vanish act? He knew he shouldn't be pursuing this. He was running a risk—the longer it went on, the more likely he was to be caught out. But as he sat near to her now, his body made up his mind for him, shoving the prickling doubt away with ease. He wanted to know her. Last night humour had sparkled in her eyes. She'd watched her friends flirt with the band with an unholy twinkle. He wanted in on her joke. And, OK, he'd lain awake the entire night harder than titanium, lusting after her again. He'd have her again right now if he could. But he was happy to do the conventional courting thing if that was how she wanted it this time. Given her all-over colour, he figured she wasn't lying when she said she didn't usually have one-night stands. So why had she? She'd been so bold. A contrary woman who had secrets. There were definitely secrets in those eyes. Rhys had secrets of his own and he was used to holding them close. But he wasn't used to others holding theirs back from him.

He inched closer, her nearness not enough. He badly wanted to feel her hair with his fingers again—glorious colour, divine length. From the way her pulse was beating, she was not immune to his proximity. He shifted again so their legs almost brushed. He had her attention. Awareness arced between them. Why did she want to run from it? 'You know, when I get close to you, you breathe a little faster.'

She nodded. 'Fear.'

'Maybe, but I don't think that's entirely true. What are you afraid of? You were fearless last night. Utterly fearless.'

She looked up at him. 'I won't say it was a mistake. But it was something that can't ever be repeated.'

His blood ran cold. 'You have a boyfriend?' He looked at her hand. 'A husband?' A ridiculous knot of jealousy pulled tight in his belly.

'No!' She flashed a hurt look at him. 'What kind of woman do you think I am?'

He relaxed, amused by her fire. 'Well, I'm not really sure. That's why I want to spend some time with you. So I can find out.'

'I'm surprised you want to spend another minute with me, you're so keen to think all these horrible things—first I'm out for a baby, then I'm cheating…'

'OK.' He held up a hand and grinned. 'Believe me, I want to spend more time with you.' She didn't soften. He needed to change tack. He ruefully rubbed his hands over his face as he tried to think of a way to break through. 'Look, let's just start over. Completely fresh. Forget all this even happened.'

'Forget *all?*'

'Let's temporarily forget last night, and totally forget the last five minutes.'

He finally got a glimmer of a smile. He leant a little closer. 'I've just sat next to you—wanting to borrow some sunscreen.'

'Sunscreen? Oh, come on, surely you can do better than that.'

He laughed. 'OK, but it's early morning and I had a sleepless night—' he gave her a meaningful look '—and it will do.' He continued with his latest façade, getting the feel for it. 'So it's sunscreen. You're a nice person, you smile, say sure, and pass me the bottle.'

'You didn't want me to rub it in for you?'

He blinked. *Hell, yes, rub right where I'm aching.* 'Let's not get ahead of ourselves again, OK?'

'Too fast?'

'A little.'

Her gurgle of laughter hit him in the solar plexus.

'Anyway, we get to chatting. We swap names. I'm Rhys and you're…'

'Sienna.'

'We chat idly. I tell you I'm here on holiday and isn't the

weather fantastic? You smile, nod, agree.' He paused, looked at her expectantly.

She laughed. 'OK. Yes, it is.'

'Finally I get around to it. I ask. Have dinner with me.'

She went back to serious.

'We're two people on holiday. Why not join forces and see some sights together? Do a little dinner. Maybe we could hit a club afterwards?' He caught her eye. She was blushing again and quickly looked away. Damn, he should've put the damper on the gas jet.

But then she spoke. 'What about lunch?'

Lunch. She was playing safe. Tortoise speed rather than hare. He figured he should be glad it wasn't 'maybe a coffee'. Right now he was happy she was still in the game. Besides, a long leisurely lunch could lead to a long lazy afternoon—or not so lazy. A chilled bottle of sauvignon blanc and seafood perhaps? They could go to...

He halted. No. He was supposed to be as much of a tourist on holiday as she was, foreign to this town. They'd have to go to a place foreign to him. Actually he'd prefer they didn't go to a restaurant at all. He wanted to keep out of the spotlight, to stay in this small stretch of beach. An idea bubbled. He answered. 'Lunch would be fantastic.'

She smiled warily. 'OK.'

It was his turn to look wary. 'So it's a date? You're not going to disappear?'

'No.' She seemed both decisive and apologetic. 'I'll be there.'

'The foyer of the hostel over the road? Midday? You're sure?'

Her smile peeked out again. 'As sure as you are.'

He couldn't hold back any longer. Reaching out, he took her hand. The fire flashed. He looked at where his skin touched hers. Looked back to her face and saw it in her serious expression. No exaggeration. The current rippled from her through every inch of his body. 'Good.'

He got away then. Needing some space to think, to plan, to perfect his new persona. He approached Reception quickly. Happy no one else was around. It was the same guy, looking ragged around the edges. He got a smile this time.

'Maitland, wanting to check out?'

'Call me Rhys. Don't you ever stop working this desk?'

He shrugged. 'I need the money.'

'I need a few more nights.'

'Sure. How many?' He tapped at the computer with a cunning smile. 'Find what you were after?'

Rhys gave him a narrow-eyed glance. 'Maybe.'

He walked out of the hostel again, straight to the taxi rank—soon in the back of a car and heading to his apartment. He pushed away the guilt with determination. Rhys Maitland didn't want to be Rhys Maitland for a couple of days. He wanted to be free and on holiday and able to do whatever— just Rhys. Maitland, Monroe, Smith—what was in a name? Justifying it because he couldn't not. He'd gone a step too far to backtrack now and he wanted to be with Sienna more than he wanted to risk being honest with her.

He stuffed a few casual clothes into a small carryall, paused when his mobile beeped. He checked it. A text from Tim.

'Where the hell r u?'

Rhys laughed. He'd forgotten about Tim and the others. He'd just gone after Sienna without thought of anything or anyone else. He was supposed to have helped pack the band's gear away. He was supposed to be at some barbecue Tim was organising for the new crop of interns this afternoon.

But now he had other plans. Better plans. He was having time out. He pushed at the buttons with his thumb.

'*On holiday.*' He sent the message, waited for the confirmation it had gone. And then, with a broad smile, he hit one last button—'*Off*'.

CHAPTER FIVE

TROUSERS were the only option. Together with the obligatory high-necked, long-sleeved top. Hell, Sienna was going to swelter. But she was going to be steaming up anyway—just from being within three feet of Mr Sex God. She took off the note wedged into the straps of her pack. Scanned it.

'We have lots of questions. We want answers. Later!'

She grinned and grimaced at the same time, then started the rummage through for some suitably unsexy outfit for her 'date'. She should have said no. She should have been rude. She should have let him think what he liked.

Impossible.

Mouth like that, eyes like those. She didn't want them frowning at her and looking icy. So she'd go. Have lunch. Do as Rhys suggested and play the game in reverse. But there'd be no re-match, pre-match or after-match frills. No resumption of body contact. But maybe she could give him the kiss goodbye she'd forgotten last night.

She pulled out her quick-dry, billion-pocketed, zip-off-leg, multi-climate, all-terrain, all-purpose pants and stared at them.

Never in a million years. Even if contact was off the menu she wasn't going looking like such a frump. They'd be great for trekking at altitude. But for a lunch in a hip Sydney café in the middle of summer? Whether accompanied by off-limits sex god or not, it was definitely a no to the trousers. Had to be a skirt. She'd go denim. It was slightly longer than the quick-dry equivalent of the combat travel pants, and no way could she wear the number from last night. Then it was just a matter of selecting which high-neck slim tee she'd team it with.

She tried to blow away the helium floating her hopes. But every breath in had them rising higher. So stupid. This was the finale—the bitter-sweet end to a fantasy come true. She sat on the bunk bed and stared into nothing.

Just go and enjoy the first half of the date that you missed out on last night. Let him see you're not some scary serial slapper or some desperate-to-get-pregnant wench. Then walk away.

Who was she kidding? It wasn't about what he thought. It was about what she wanted—more time in his company. And it wasn't just that he oozed a raw sexuality that had her hot in the ping of a bra strap. She didn't just want him, she wanted to get to know him. There was more going on in those greeny-grey eyes that she wanted to explore.

Exactly midday she left the room and went downstairs, met his gaze across the foyer. He was over by the reception desk watching as she descended the last few steps. He made her feel as if she were supermodel beautiful, as if the eyes of the world were on her—watching, wanting. No one had ever looked that way at her before. Everyone had always *known*. For once she was centre-stage, not in the wings—actively involved rather than in the audience.

She walked up to him as with deliberation he looked her up and down and back up again. Ordinarily his mouth held sensual promise; right now, the smile stretching it was utterly carnal. She had no idea if anyone else was around, all she could see was him, all she could sense was the force of his presence, his breadth, the awareness crackling so near the surface. He looked up the length of her legs once more and the desire in his eyes had her wobbling. Deep inside her body was soft and hot and aching with emptiness. But the pounding of her heart reminded her. That look in his eyes would be snuffed out the instant he saw her scar. He might lie, as Neil had, and say it made no difference. But it would make every difference—he wouldn't treat her as real any more. She broke the eye contact, looked down to the ground, registered the big red chilly bin beside him.

He finally tore his eyes from her legs and nudged the bin with his foot. 'Tell me you like seafood.'

'I like seafood.'

'Really?'

She nodded.

'Good. Should have asked earlier.'

'We're having a picnic?'

'That OK? I thought it was such a great day…' He trailed off, attention back on her legs.

She clamped her upper thighs together, halting the warm urge to swing them open, and managed a cool friendly smile. 'That's great.'

She took the blanket that rested on top of the container. Hugged it in a protective hold. He took the chilly. They crossed the road and wandered down to the beach. Hunted out a nice spot to park their burdens and themselves.

She was glad of the crowds. Glad of the broadness of the daylight—because she seriously needed to get a grip. When he was with her she had the crazy feeling that anything was possible. And it wasn't. He didn't know about her. And when he did, everything would change. Better for him never to know so she didn't have to witness that change. Better to end it before it began. He'd been right—this was just the beginning, but of a fantasy. She would have to finish it so she could treasure it for ever—before it turned into a nightmare.

He set up the umbrella that had been strapped to the side of the chilly.

'You've gone to a lot of trouble in a short time.'

He grinned. 'Not at all. The umbrella is from the hostel. I bought the chilly bin from the store down the road and the food is from a great seafood market I found. They packed everything.'

She spread the blanket for them to sit. She was glad she'd gone with the skirt option. Even though the umbrella shaded them, the temperature was still hitting hot—her internal heat going way higher.

'Drink?' He'd unscrewed the lid off a bottle of sauvignon blanc, deftly holding two glasses in one hand while pouring the wine into them.

She glanced at him, catching his eyes for the first time since leaving the hostel, read the challenge.

'Thank you.'

Her fingers touched his as he gave her the glass. With more luck than skill, she managed not to drop it. All that raced through her head was the memory of those fingers brushing across her back.

Sensible speech was impossible. So she asked a few meaningless, ice-breaker questions. Barely heard his meaningless, ice-breaker answers. Relief came as he unwrapped the food—a fabulous platter of deep-sea delicacies. He piled a few chunks of French bread on a plate, added a swipe of butter to each.

Cool, tasty, satisfying. The succulent seafood slipped down her throat—mussels, prawns, shredded lobster. He handed her an oyster, artfully sitting in its half shell. He winked.

A spurt of mirth bubbled in her. 'Are you trying to feed me aphrodisiacs?'

He laughed aloud. 'I'm doing everything in my power to seduce you.'

He'd already done that. And she'd succumb again this minute if there were any way to maintain the level of excitement and enjoyment evident in his eyes. He was out for a little holiday fun—that was obvious. And if only she was truly able to escape her history, she'd do the same.

They ate, talked a little more, looked a lot more—he was so handsome, she couldn't help but stare, until she could no longer take the need slicing through her. She concentrated instead on the beach volleyball game a few yards away, amazed the women actually managed to stay decent in the teensy, eensy, weensy minuscule strips of Lycra that they passed off as their bikinis. They must use tape. Had to.

He was watching her, amusement apparent. 'You want to play?'

'Oh, no.'

'No?'

'I'm not good with ball games.' Never played. Never allowed. Always on the sidelines while her overprotective mother and brother told her she couldn't and shouldn't. Consequently she was hopeless and not about to show him and a beach full of others how bad she was at catching a ball.

His amusement had increased—he wasn't in on her teen angst.

'Really?' His mind seemed to have gone in another direction entirely. 'You know, if you want, I can give you some help with that.'

She looked at him.

His grin was wicked. 'Ball skills.'

She cleared her throat, narrowed her eyes at him but ducked the challenge. 'I didn't do team sports as a kid.'

'No?' He let it slide. 'What did you do?'

'I was in the orchestra—percussion.'

'You were the girl clanging the cymbal, huh?'

She giggled. 'Yeah, waiting the entire length of the piece for my one moment of glory.'

Much like now. And the satisfaction couldn't be repeated.

'So no team sports. Were you a runner or something? Track and field?'

She laughed aloud. Her mirth rather more than the question merited.

'I'm guessing no, then. But you're fit. You're very fit.'

She nodded. She liked feeling strong. She'd taken years to get strong. 'Yoga.'

'Really?'

'Yeah. And Pilates, Thai Chi. All sorts, really. Anything good for strength and flexibility.'

'Flexibility?' He drew in an audible breath. 'Interesting.'

She paused, aware of the extra charge in the already electric air. He was looking at her legs again. She could almost see into his mind. See the mental movie he was playing there.

The atmosphere was so humid and heavy not even a scimitar sword would slice it. Breathing utterly impossible. With great deliberation, and sheer force of will, she turned and stared at the volleyball players some more.

This had been a terrible idea. How had she thought she could seriously sit and lunch with the sexiest guy ever to walk the earth and rein in temptation? Especially when he was making it more than clear that he wanted to tempt.

But he started chatting again. Asking idle questions that had her answering, soft laughter ensuing, relaxing. God, she needed to find a reason not to like him. And fast. But he was making it impossible with his warm eyes, attentive, listening close. Quite some time passed before she realised she wasn't getting to know anything much about him—other than that he looked fantastic in long shorts. He was all questions, all ears, not offering up a lot of himself in return. Usually she was the listener, the one steering the conversation with questions and open-ended comments. She liked it, liked learning about other people, what made them tick, what made them the way they were. She decided to ask a few questions of her own.

'What are you doing on holiday here?'

He shrugged. 'I needed a complete change.'

'Catching up with old friends?'

He looked confused for a moment. 'Oh, Tim. Yeah. A mate from school.'

The book titled Rhys was closed again. Still not much info to process. She looked at him, trying to read more from his expression. But, although friendly, he was guarded. There were secrets in there. Well, OK, she had a few too, but this was simply the conclusion to a wonderful night—she wasn't asking for his deepest thoughts or fears. Couldn't he be a little more forthcoming?

And then he smiled. She couldn't help but notice his mouth again. He had such an advantage. That smile, those lips. The green in his eyes sharpened. She ran a light hand over her forehead, tried to remember what she'd been going to ask him.

He leant towards her. 'Feeling the heat?'

Just a tad.

'Want to go for a swim?'

Yeah, right. Splashing with him in the waves? Visions of them lying in the surf at the shore, limbs entwined like in some old Hollywood movie, rolled in her head. But there was a huge crowd at the beach now. And sand itched. And she'd have to reveal the very thing she wanted to conceal.

'I don't have my swimsuit on.'

'Damn, I was hoping to get you in your bikini.'

Definitely not going there. 'I don't wear a bikini. Don't want to get too much sun.'

He looked at her tanned legs, brows slightly raised.

Doh. She blandly stared him out.

Finally he shrugged. 'Well, as it can't be a swim, I'm going to go get us an ice cream.'

He rose, long limbs lazily moving with innate grace. She watched him walk towards the vendor over on the footpath, then lay back on the blanket, absurdly at ease in spite of the insane awareness. She enjoyed the faint scent of him left in the air, glanced down at the dent in the sand where his legs had rested. The warmth of the sun, the satisfaction from that delicious lunch, had a soporific effect. The sleeplessness of the night before had its after-effect now. Drowsy, she closed her eyes. Relaxed. She thought of him, of what could have been if things were different. Dreamed dangerously pleasant dreams.

'Hey, sleepy.'

He'd returned. She smiled. Kept her eyes closed. Wanting to extend the fantasy for a few more moments. She heard the scrunch of sand as he sat. She felt something cold touch her mouth. She licked her lips, tasted the creamy ice.

'Nice?' His voice sounded very near, very low, very husky.

'Yes.' Her tongue traversed her lower lip again.

'More?' Even lower, even huskier.

'Yes.'

His warm finger daubed cold ice on her mouth.

He muttered. 'You mind sharing?'

She didn't get the chance to reply. Only to sigh faintly as his tongue flicked the sweetness from her. She sent her tongue out to meet his. She couldn't resist his kiss. Just a little more of a man who wanted her in a way she'd never been wanted before. His fingers went to her jaw, turning her face towards his. She opened her mouth. Let him in. Their tongues met and mated and a tempting touch became total turn-on. Deep, hungry kisses that felt divine and promised even greater pleasure could come. She didn't want him ever to stop kissing her, didn't want to stop kissing him. The sensual caresses drove everything from her mind. Only this, only him. She lifted her hand, combing fingers into his hair, holding him so she could kiss him back as fiercely as he was kissing her.

Her curves melted into his hard planes, her body instinctively recognising his muscles. The way they felt around her, their strength at holding her. Making her his prisoner and his keeper. His hot body lay close; he threw his knee across hers. Teasingly heavy. She wanted the rest of his weight over her. She couldn't prevent the parting of her legs, couldn't stop the arch of her pelvis towards him. She moaned into his mouth.

She wanted. Wanted, wanted, wanted…

His hand came to rest on her lower belly, pressing on her, the weight a tiny taste of the delight of having his whole body over hers. His fingers spread on the flat of her stomach. Smoothing upwards. Skin on…*skin.*

She pulled back sharply. Flashed open her eyes. Stared up at him in horror as she saw him looking down the length of her body. No, no and no again.

She wrenched out of his hold, sitting up and scooting away. His surprise was total.

'Sienna?'

'I'm sorry. I can't. I'm really sorry.' Her heart thudded. Her eyes threatened to spill tears of apology and frustration. 'I really am sorry.'

* * *

Rhys watched her run across the sand and swore sharply enough for the family group several feet away to turn around and frown at him. He felt a vague flush, slid back under the shade of the umbrella and strove for control. Anger, frustration and plain shock hit him. She'd done it again. Run out on him. Hell, was she some kind of warped tease?

Instinct told him no. She'd felt genuine desire, genuine regret. Well, damn if she didn't owe him an explanation—again. He packed away the remnants of the picnic with precise movements, then headed for the hostel.

He walked straight into the dorm room he now knew to be hers. There seemed to be a mass of women hanging there. They turned and stared at him as if he were an invading Martian. But Rhys was well used to walking into a room full of women—at the nurses' stations, or the new interns. Addressing a bunch of women who were sending a variety of looks from under their lashes wasn't something that intimidated or really even interested him. What interested him was that one woman.

'Is Sienna here?' He addressed them collectively.

'Sure is.' He recognised the speaker as one of the friends at the bar the night before.

It was like the parting of the Red Sea. He looked where they separated and to where she sat on a bottom bunk, quiet and red-faced. Her annoyance and embarrassment were obvious and, yes, her upset. What was she afraid of? Surely not him?

She stood. 'Rhys, you can't come in here.'

'Bet you want to, though, don't you?' The South African again. Caustic delivery.

Rhys ignored the stifled giggles. Time to turn on the charm. He was a Maitland—had the genes, the upbringing.

He might loathe it but public speaking was a skill he could call on.

'I'm sorry to butt in on you ladies, but I need to explain something to my friend here.' He didn't take his eyes off Sienna, but sensed the slight hostility in the room. It was as clear to them as it was to him that she was feeling edgy and that he was the cause. He needed to claim back some points— penitent man would be a good start. 'You see—' he gave a small shrug '—I owe her an apology.' He didn't know what for yet but they didn't need to know that.

All seven heads swivelled to Sienna. He felt the atmosphere soften.

'You want to say sorry?'

'Yeah. I'd say it all right now but I need some time with her to explain things properly. Alone.'

He swallowed his smile at her obvious discomfort. Her big blues were fixed on him and the incredulity warring with anger was unbelievably amusing.

'This is way better than any movie.' A different South African this time, she got a low murmur of agreement.

Sienna's cheeks were redder than a fire engine. 'Stop it, Rhys.' She addressed the girls. 'It's me who owes the apology. Again.' Contrite eyes pleaded with him and the rest of the room. Hmm. She was good. A little honesty mixed in with a sidestep.

She turned back to him. 'I'm sorry, Rhys.'

He heard the finality she was striving for and tensed. He wasn't about to let her go. 'Let's get coffee and talk.'

'I can't now. I've promised to go to an art gallery with Brooke this afternoon.'

He was not letting her slip away a third time—he'd have his answers. 'That's OK. You can make it up to me later.' He studied the now silent audience. They could be more of a help to him than her if he played it right. 'Don't you think she should?' He cast a soulful gaze around; it wasn't much of a stretch to play the part of crushed suitor—not hard at all given he actually felt it.

'Oh, yeah, Sienna. You must.'

He had them now, eating out of his palm.

'Give the guy a break.'

'She'll see you later at that bar.' Caustic South African again. More on his side than he'd realised. 'We'll make sure she's there. Six p.m. Have her drink waiting.'

'Yes, ma'am.'

He didn't stick around to let Sienna try to argue, but her eyes flashed her thoughts in the final moment he met them. Anxiety, anger, reluctance—and, at the bottom of it all, desire.

CHAPTER SIX

SIENNA didn't go to the gallery. She went shopping. She was pathetic. But she wanted him again so badly and she wanted it to be as good as the night before. So she was on a mission for a new top—anything that might work. She stopped at the make-up counter. Stage make-up could create a fabulous scar—couldn't it hide one too? She tried on a variety of in-season style tops. There was none with a polo neck. Everything was summery—low-cut and revealing. Exactly what she didn't want.

In despair she went to the lingerie section of the department store. New frillies were supposed to help with confidence, weren't they?

'How was the gallery?' Rhys was waiting. Clad in jeans and a different shirt. Cool beer in a glass, half empty already. Steely eyes lanced her with questions that she knew he wouldn't hold back on. That she knew she was going to have to answer. Honestly.

'I didn't go. Went shopping instead.'

'Buy anything interesting?'

'No.' A new bra. She was wearing it now. Figured if she was going to go down she might as well do it in a hot outfit.

And her sensible travel numbers didn't have the requisite lace ratio. This one did. She could feel her budded nipples pressing against the slightly scratchy stitching even now.

'Sienna—'

She didn't want to be here. Didn't want the pretence. Didn't want the girls from the hostel, whom she hardly knew, watching and wondering. This was going to end in tears—for her anyway. She might as well just get it over with right now.

She grabbed him by the hand. 'Let's get out of here.'

He let her lead, walking beside her but in the direction of her choice. She marched down the street not having a clue where she was headed. Just wanting away from eyes and those memories only recently made but that were going to be the best of a lifetime. Right now she was going to ruin them.

The contact of his hand around hers meant her blood was travelling at high speed to every outlying inch. Making her feel more aware of her body, making her feel more alive than she ever had. It didn't frighten her. It seduced her. Frustration and want and bitterness forced her. She wanted him enough to risk it.

She went into the alleyway a shop down from the hostel. Ducked into a doorway partly along. Turned to face him. He was right behind her.

'Sienna?'

She shut him up with her mouth, passionately pressing against him. His arms clamped around her. He pivoted to lean against the door, taking her weight with him. Hot, intense, searing kisses—as if the moment on the beach had never been interrupted, only intensified. Burning, aching, she swept her hands across his shoulders, rotated against him, driving her hips against his. Wanting to reconnect, taking his mouth with a depth of passion she relished and wanted to relive again and again.

He jerked his head back. 'What the *hell* is going on, Sienna?'

She pulled him back to her. Not wanting to think. Not wanting to admit to anything just yet. Wanting to drown her doubts for moments longer in his kiss.

'You want this?' He groaned against her. 'You want me? Say it.'

'Yes.' She clawed him closer. 'I want you.'

His fingers pulled in her hair, holding her still so he could plunder, pressing a hard kiss that left her in no doubt of the frustration he'd been feeling all afternoon. A kiss that left her utterly without breath.

The lack of oxygen, the fever, sent her crazy. She reached for him. Reckless. If she'd been able to get away with it once, couldn't she do it again? If she could somehow keep his hands occupied—like the way she had last night, forcing him to take her weight, to take her. God, she wanted that again. His strength. His glorious width. Frantic, furious and fast. She fought with his belt. Once more. Just once.

He pulled back sharply, grabbing her hands, stopping them with his. 'No.'

She looked up at him in surprise. Stepped back when she saw the anger in his eyes.

He shook his head at her. 'Too fast.' A savage whisper.

She tried to get her hands back but he tightened his grip. 'If we're going to do this, we're going to do this properly.' He eyeballed her, stepping closer. 'My room or yours?'

She looked away. Damn. Honestly she wanted nothing more than to lie in a comfortable bed and be able to explore him freely and at leisure, but it wouldn't be the same. He'd be like Neil— freeze, then run a mile. Or he'd treat her like some fragile piece of glass and she hated being wrapped in cotton wool.

He stepped even closer, so his body pressed against hers. His erection teased her. His question terrified her. 'Why won't you let me see you naked?'

She tried to pull away but he moved closer still—pushing her back against the wall, keeping hold of her hands, his body leaning into hers.

Her breathing shallowed—half from fear, half from desire.

'You're willing to let me kiss you. You're willing to let me *inside* you. But you won't take your clothes off.'

'Rhys…' Amazed at his acuteness, she pleaded with him not to go there despite knowing it had been inevitable—from the moment he'd strode onto the sand beside her this morning. She'd been kidding herself to think she could get away with not telling him. But it was exactly what she didn't want to have happened. Exactly why she'd run into the night after their encounter.

'Why?'

She stared into his searching eyes, at his sensual mouth now pulled into a hard line. She reached up on tiptoe, pressed her hand to his lips. Finally felt them soften and part. He kissed the tip of her fingers—his mouth moving slowly, warm and teasing.

Desire raged through her veins, coupled with painful anger over what was to come. But she knew no matter what happened, no matter how things would change, she couldn't walk away from him a third time. She was as human as the next person and the temptation was too strong. She had to run the risk so she could have the chance of feeling his erotic intensity again.

She pulled her hand away. He straightened, watching her, waiting for her answer.

She stared at his shirt buttons. 'I have a scar.'

There was a bit of a silence.

'So do I.'

She jerked her head up.

He looked down at her. Mouth twitching. 'You show me yours, I'll show you mine.'

She stared back at him and watched his humorous touch fade. His brows lifted. 'Big scar?'

'Pretty big.' Actually it wasn't. More like hairline, it was what it represented that was huge.

'It can't be as big as mine.' He firmed his grip on her.

He still wasn't getting it. Unable to handle it any more, she grabbed the neckline of her tee in a tight fist. Pulled it down so it exposed the vee of skin all the way from her neck down to the dainty bow decorating the point where the cups of her bra met in the middle. The scar ran from the base of her throat. A straight line right down the centre of her body. Defining her.

She saw the shock register in his face. And recognition. And then she saw it. The look she'd known was unavoidable. Fear. He hid it quickly. Shutting down. Closing off. But it had been there. She tensed.

He said nothing. Just stood frozen. Staring at her chest. His mouth opened a fraction and the buttons on his shirt jumped about as she heard the sharp intake of breath.

Anger and pride held her head high. Her chin lifted higher—underlining the challenge he'd already failed. As she'd predicted, as she'd known, the flame of desire was snuffed out in a flash.

She pushed him back against the wall. Met no resistance, almost as if he'd stepped back at the moment she pushed. She ran, feet light in her sandals. She didn't look back. She didn't need to. He didn't come after her. Didn't call out. Didn't seem to stir even.

She dragged in deep breaths, pushing the sobs back deep into her chest. *Forget it, forget it, forget it.*

She scurried past Curtis on Reception, raced into the telly room, knowing at this time on a Saturday night it was bound to be empty, everyone would be out partying. She chose a big chair on the far side of the room, curled into it like a cat, hiding from the world. She reached into her small day pack and pulled out her journal.

The list of wannabe life achievements she'd scrawled on page one stared at her, making a fool of her. She told herself it didn't matter. Tried not to let it ruin everything. Failed. With anger and misery she relived past revelations.

Neil had been like that. Backed off the instant he'd seen it. Eventually he'd returned. But he'd been hesitant, treating her gingerly. Then he'd made it worse. He'd told the world. She'd only just escaped her hometown and the notoriety of being the 'heart-girl'. Wanting to start over with anonymity. Be normal, like anyone else at university. She'd thought she could trust Neil to see past it. He didn't. And her secret had become common knowledge—the looks, unwanted, undeserved pity sent her way again. And rather than understanding more, Neil had understood less. Become more protective, more and more stifling until he was as bad as her mother and brother combined.

She wanted freedom. She wanted to be the same as anyone else—and to be treated like that. Part of the reason she was going overseas was to start over—again. She read over the list again. Then, for the first time in all her years of keeping a journal, she ripped a page right out.

Rhys rested back on the warm bricks as a range of emotions rushed through him. Shock, anger and desire but mostly disappointment. In himself—what had happened to his renowned beside manner? His unflappable charm? So much for an uncomplicated summer fling. He'd known what he was looking at. For a second after the shock he'd even admired the skill of the surgeon who'd done it. As neat a job as you could get. Then the ramifications set in. You got that kind of scar from a major operation. Open-heart surgery. The thought of her lying on an operating table had made him recoil. Not someone as young and full of vitality as her.

Stupid, when every day at the hospital he was confronted with mortality—he knew full well it could hit anyone any time. He knew that from his own brush with it as a kid. With Theo.

He hadn't been joking about having a scar of his own. It was a mess, but it had left an even bigger mess on the inside. While Sienna's heart might have been operated on, his was the scarred one—one that had never fully healed. He tried so hard to make it right. And failed every time. Roughly healed, puckered tissue formed a protective barrier and he didn't want anyone to penetrate it. He wasn't going to be vulnerable. He'd never reveal the depth of that pain—to anyone. Nor did he want to set himself up for more of that kind of hurt.

He headed back to the hostel. Maybe he should just check out. She'd be feeling pretty mad with him and he was mad with her for not giving him a chance. For springing it on him and then skipping out.

But the more he thought of her, the greater his need to see her again grew. As the shock faded, he felt the resurgence of desire. If anything he wanted her more. He wanted to kiss away the pain he'd seen in her eyes. He wanted them heavy with passion and the glow of life. He refused to analyse why. Just pegged it on desire. Tim had told him to lighten up, to take a break. He rationalised, remembered she was only in town for a few days. This could still be a holiday fling. They weren't talking for ever and babies. Being with her once more couldn't do him any more damage—or her. Maybe they could both forget about their scars for a while.

Curtis was in his regular position behind the reception desk. 'Did they concrete you in place here?' Rhys muttered.

Curtis looked up from the old gossip mag in front of him,

his eyes narrowing when he saw it was Rhys. 'She's in the TV room. Looks like you're in trouble.'

Rhys acknowledged the truth with a grunt and went in search of her. He looked into the room, saw her in the far corner, her fine-boned figure folded into the armchair. Her head jerked up as he approached and he saw her stuff a piece of paper into her book, snap it shut and then jam the whole thing into her bag.

'You running out on me is a really bad habit.'

'Be honest, this time you were happy to be run out on.'

'No, I wasn't, and I really don't want you to run out on me again.'

She stared up at him, the blue in her eyes shadowed with the purple of pain. Looking all the more intense in the unnatural pallor of her face.

He boxed on. 'I never did get to show you my scar. You walked away before I had the chance.'

'You froze over. Colder than, than…'

'I was unprepared.'

'It's good that way. Then I get an honest reaction.'

'It's not fair to set someone up. What was I supposed to do? Of course I was going to be shocked. How could I have predicted that? Anyway, it looks to me like some kind of life-saving scar.'

She looked away from him then, seeming to focus on a speck of dust hanging in mid-air.

'Did it work?'

'Clearly.'

He hid his smile at her caustic tone. 'Come on.' He tugged on her hand, hauling her out of the chair. 'I've got something to show you.'

'Rhys, I really don't want—'

'Come with me.' He spoke quickly and then gave a cheeky grin as he realised the *double entendre* of his words.

She looked less bruised, more baleful.

'Please.' He kept hold of her hand and led her up the stairs, away from Curtis' grin and to the privacy of his own room.

'You know, yours isn't really much of a scar. Mine is much bigger.'

She blinked. He'd taken her aback. He undid his jeans and pushed them down so he could step out of them. He hadn't bothered with boxers so his erection thrust up. He suppressed his satisfaction as he saw her eyes widen at the sight of him. Her deadened look disappeared. Her cheeks flushed. Yes, he still wanted her. Now she knew it.

He twisted his leg to show her the place on the outside of his thigh where the glass had gone deep. The scar was old and jagged but still angry-looking.

She was totally diverted. Frowning at it. 'That's not a life-saving scar.'

'No.' It had been a life-taking scar. A constant reminder to him of that day of youthful folly and painful helplessness. The kind of day he'd determined never to experience again. The mistakes he'd never repeat, the inability to do a damn thing…

'I don't really want to talk about it either.' He pulled back his leg. 'So, I win on the scar stakes.' He shut out the memories, shut away the emotion. No room for that kind of emotion here. Only fun—a fling with the sexiest woman he'd ever seen.

They'd just forget their wounds for a few moments. He reached out to her, touching his fingers to the back of her hand, sliding up her arm, stepping closer. But she held back, stiff, head away, not melting into his embrace. He thought he knew why. So they weren't going to be able to forget the scars just yet—at least not hers. He kissed the corner of her mouth. Spoke right into her ear.

'Sienna, for the record. You are not ugly. Your scar is not ugly.'

'I don't think I'm ugly.' She pulled back and he saw vehemence in her eyes. 'That's not what worries me. It's more that people take one look and start acting like I'm going to collapse in a corner any moment. When I wear a low-cut top, I see their curiosity. People look at me, then quickly look away thinking either I'm a circus exhibit or I'm on borrowed time.'

'And are you?'

'Well, I might be able to do the splits but it's going to take me years to learn to juggle.'

'You can do the splits?'

The big blues glinted back at him. 'Three ways.'

'OK, you can prove that to me later, but for now you're saying you're not a circus exhibit and you're not going to collapse in the corner in the next five minutes?'

'You got it.'

He waited, knowing there was more. Despite the gentle humour she wasn't ready yet and he wanted to hear all she had to say.

She stumbled her way through it. 'Last night…last night was amazing.'

'Yes.' He agreed quietly—major understatement.

'You didn't know.'

He thought for a second, trying to figure where she was going—she thought it was amazing only because he didn't know? 'You think it's going to change now I do?'

The flush in her cheeks deepened but she looked him square in the eye—he found himself understanding the expression 'true blue' precisely, such was the painful honesty reflected there. 'I just want to fully enjoy everything like normal people do,' she mumbled.

He started to see even clearer. 'You don't want any soft treatment because of your history.'

She nodded.

'You want to be just like anybody else.'

She nodded again.

He chuckled. 'I'm sorry, honey, but there is no way on this earth you'll ever be just like anybody else.' He finished his thought before her mad look got madder. 'You're special.' Very special and his body was harder than it had ever been. He asked, 'Do you want to be pushed to extremes, Sienna?'

She stared. 'What sort of extremes?' She sucked in a breath as if she were tasting fresh mountain air for the first time. 'Like last night sort of extreme?'

It was his turn to nod—slowly. 'Yeah.' He slid his hands to her hips, wanting to keep her near him. 'Shall we find out exactly how much pleasure your body is capable of?'

The shiver shook her from head to foot. Huge blue pools stared up at him, mirroring her thoughts—incredulity at what he'd said, excitement, temptation.

He couldn't quite believe he'd said it himself, but now he had, he knew it was exactly what she needed. And what he needed—the most wonderful challenge. The opportunity to forget himself, his life, and just bury deep into her, make her forget the trauma her body had been through, show her how much fun she could have.

He saw the moment she was sold—the flash in her eyes, the parting of her mouth.

'OK.'

He hugged her, holding her close to the beat in his own chest, savouring the satisfaction in knowing she wouldn't be running out on him again, that he'd have all the time he needed to quench this lust. Thank God they were finally in agreement.

No one had ever stared at her before with such a look of want. Did he really not mind it? Did he even notice it? Did he not wonder?

'Is it OK if I touch it?'

So he definitely saw it. He ran his finger down the white line that bisected her from base of her throat to diaphragm. Then he looked to the side. He grinned. 'Is it OK if I touch these?' He cupped her breasts; his thumbs stroked her nipples through her bra. 'Very pretty. Pretty flowers, but what's underneath is even prettier.' He pulled the lace down so her nipples played peek-a-boo over the top. Bent and pressed kisses along the rising slope of one, stopped just shy of her nipple—it was so hard it hurt. He slid his hands around her back, loosened the catch and let the straps fall from her shoulders.

'Extreme…' he muttered. 'Let's see if we can do extreme.'

She held her breath, refusing to let her body sway towards his, one last doubt needing to be dealt with. 'I don't frighten you?'

He laughed. 'A slim little thing like you?'

'No.' She jabbed a finger at her chest. 'This doesn't frighten you?'

'Honestly?' He stared straight into her eyes. 'No.' He grazed the back of his knuckles against her nipples. 'I'll tell you what frightens me. The thought of not having you for one whole night where I can lie with you and we can go at it like rabbits.'

She giggled, spontaneous effervescence bursting through her solemnity. 'How do rabbits do it?'

'I don't know but they do it lots. Let's just go with the lots for now, OK?'

'OK.'

He pulled his tee shirt over his head. Then he returned to her breasts, finally fitting that heaven-sent mouth around her pointed tip and letting his tongue rough over it.

She marvelled at the feel of his hands on her body, the way

he was struggling with his passion. He really wasn't fazed by her scar at all—his desire not lessened by any degree. If anything he was even more aroused than the night before. She figured that was because, in one way, he didn't care. He just wanted her. Wasn't worried for her. Because there was nothing invested here—they weren't talking futures or relationships or anything remotely serious. Hell, they weren't even talking tomorrow. They were talking sex—good, hard sex, right now.

That was OK. In fact, she reasoned in the last seconds she could still think, that was perfect—they were living life right in this moment. Exactly how she'd decided she had to live. No guarantees, just go with the now.

He undid the button on her skirt and tugged at it, his fingers catching her panties underneath as well. Slowly, he slid his hands down, kneeling before her as he pulled both skirt and underwear off.

'You have the most magnificent legs I have ever seen.'

She looked down. Six foot three of strongly muscled, extremely naked man was at her feet and gazing at her with unconcealed lust—despite her scar. She was as naked as he. The answering desire inspired in her meant she could hardly stand. She reached a shaking hand out to his shoulder, needing the support.

He stood, scooped her up. 'Do you have any idea the thoughts I've had these last twenty-four hours?'

She let her head fall back on his chest, willingly doing the featherweight female act. 'Do I want to?'

'Sure you do. But—' he grinned as he spread her on the bed to his satisfaction '—I'm not going to tell you, I'm just going to do it.'

He started with a kiss that tasted of his smile and his promise of maximum pleasure. She kissed him back, hungry to take the satisfaction she knew he'd give. His determination, his intention, was unmistakable and she was breathless with just the thought of it, let alone the accomplishment.

He left her lips, left her gasping, while he kissed her cheeks, her jaw, down her neck—kissing all over her shoulders and chest until her entire torso had been touched by his beautiful mouth. His hands worked in accompaniment—trailing fire, teasing, tending to the parts of her that his mouth wasn't fixed to. Meantime she tried to take in air.

He slid down the bed, between legs she'd happily parted. He placed one knee over his shoulder, so he could kiss along the inside of her leg. 'That OK for you?'

Nothing beat the sensation of his stubble gently rasping against her inner thighs. 'Uh-huh.'

He lifted her other leg over his other shoulder so his head was cradled between her thighs. She was hot and wet and he hadn't even touched her yet—not there. She could hardly wait. She raised her hips, wanting to rock them, wanting him to rub and rotate and reach right into her.

His lips curved and her desire to have them press against her became paramount. 'Rhys.'

He bent his head and she stopped breathing altogether. When she started again, it was even faster and shallower. Her entire body beat to the pulse of his movements, to the rhythm of the blood in her veins. She'd never lain like this. Never wanted anything or anyone the way she wanted him doing this, like this.

His fingers stroked, his mouth teased. And all the while she got hotter and wetter and way more vocal about what she wanted—for once in her life she had someone listening, who was willing to take her where she wanted to go at the speed she wanted to go at. She was on the journey and he was the chauffeur. She called out, encouraging him, so close.

He raised his head. 'Need to slow down a second, honey.'

Why?

His half-smile at her expression inflamed her. When he gave her the reason he nearly sent her over the edge. 'I want you really ready.'

She was ready alright. She was beyond ready.

Suddenly he rose, kneeling, hands on her calves. As if she were a doll, he scissored her legs, pushing one right above her head. He looked intrigued. 'You weren't kidding about the splits.'

She grinned and shook her head. Pliant, she stretched for him. He wound her other leg around his waist. The position had her so exposed. His hand hardened round her ankle, the look on his face intensified as he gazed down the length of her leg with wicked intent. Aroused beyond bearing, she could hardly stand the wait.

He arched over, bringing his hips into line with hers. 'This is going to be as deep as it can get. That OK?'

Of course it was OK. She was just damn glad she'd done all that yoga and had no problems with flexibility. 'Yeah.'

He edged in a fraction and then, with his other hand pressing on the mattress beside her hip, penning her in place, he caught her eye and thrust fiercely.

She cried out. Deep wasn't the word.

His eyes narrowed; she could see the tension in his jaw. 'OK?'

She nodded. More than OK. More than anything she'd ever known. Her body half lifted off the bed with him as he tilted back, pausing before pushing in again.

She couldn't hold back the whimper—of delight and of desire. This was incredible.

'You want physical, Sienna?' He gulped in air. 'I can do physical.'

She picked up what he'd left unsaid. 'Just physical?'

He puffed out. 'Yeah.'

Fine. At least he was honest. Besides, she'd be gone in a week, and she was living *right now.* 'So do it.'

He didn't need telling again. Slowly, but with the impact of a ten-tonne truck, he surged into her, grinding deep before pulling back inch by devastating inch.

She'd never been so totally possessed. She couldn't move, couldn't even embrace him back, instead she reached her arms up above her head and took hold of the railing of the headboard—trying to keep as in control as him but with every deep, powerful thrust he took a little more from her.

'You like it?'

'Yes.'

'Want more?'

'Yes.'

'Harder?'

'Yes.'

And from then she couldn't speak, could only moan and not even do that consciously. All she could see was him. All she could feel was him—he was touching her innermost core, and it was so sensitive, so exquisite, she honestly thought she couldn't cope. The heat in her body was so intense she shied from it, shook her head, wanting it to stop, never wanting it to stop.

He spoke. Growled at her as he slowly pulled out. 'Give me that fearless response I had last night. You don't want fear from me—well, I don't want fear from you either.'

He pushed harder on her leg, parting her further so she was so open, so that each time his body slammed forward as much of him entered her as was physically possible—and then some. His pace increased and her consciousness receded. His pelvic bone rubbed against hers—tormenting her, bringing her closer and closer to an oblivion she couldn't contend with.

She held tighter to the rail. She couldn't take it, couldn't...

'More?' His hand gripped, his muscles bunched, his expression showed his thin grip on his self-command.

She couldn't resist. Gave in to the overwhelming instinct to surrender. 'Yes. Oh...'

He pounded. She lost it. Closed her eyes against him, screwed them tight in the agony of ecstasy, her scream sounding around the room.

His body locked rigid as he uttered one word before giving in to the tension, the demand to drive deep and hard that one last time and pour his all into her.

'Perfect.'

CHAPTER SEVEN

'WE NEED to rest a while.' Rhys reached down to the side of the bed, brought back up a bottle of water and held it for Sienna to sip before drinking deep himself. He caught her eye and winked. 'Not bad.'

She lay, gasping for air, wondering if she'd ever catch her breath again. Knowing that when she did, she was asking him to do that again. And again. Blood pounded through her body, singing through her veins. She'd never felt so alive.

'Tell me about it now.'

'The scar?'

He nodded.

Why hold back? He hadn't been lying when he'd said she didn't scare him. He'd just taken her apart and put her back together and shown her she worked just fine. She could tell him it all, knowing he wasn't going to treat her any different—he'd proved that magnificently. 'I was born with a heart condition. My valves didn't work properly and eventually I had to have a couple replaced.'

'Valves?'

She nodded.

He nodded with her. 'How did they find out about it?'

'My dad died from a heart condition when I was little. He

was young—it was really hard on my mum. She got worried that my brother and I might have inherited a weak heart. So she got us checked out and they found it.' She grimaced. 'Then it was all on.'

'What was on?'

She understood the way her mother had reacted, why she'd gone so over the top—she'd never got over her husband's death. She didn't want to lose another of her loved ones. Seeing her pain had made Sienna's decisions for her own future—she couldn't control how Jake and her mother felt, but she could stop how other people felt about her. She refused to burden anyone else with that kind of worry, that heartache. And she refused to let anyone else try to restrict her life the way they had hers— even with the best of intentions. Her relationship with Neil had cemented that decision. It had proved she couldn't have it all. So no long-term relationships, no marriage. Certainly no kids. She didn't want them to inherit this crummy heart. It was the price she'd pay to have the freedom to do as she wanted.

'Mum was terrified she'd lose me. She had a terrible time losing Dad. I know she didn't mean to but her fear made my life a nightmare. So did Jake—my brother. I understand it, I do. But they were so restrictive, totally overprotective. And everyone knew about it. It defined me. Seems like that was who I was, that was all I was. The girl with the dodgy ticker.'

She pulled the sheet up, covering her cooling body. 'I was at the doctor's my whole life. Second opinions, check-ups— any hint of something as little as a cold and I was packed off to the damn doctor—again and again and again. Sidelined from all the fun things.' She paused to draw breath so she could speak with greater force. 'I hated it. Hated them. Constant prodding. Constant questions. Telling you what you can and can't do—all the time. Not that Mum listened too close anyway—she only heard the can't not the can.'

She got a grip on her emotion, tried to look to the future. 'I've had the operation now. I've got my degree. I'm well and strong and I want to move on.'

She still disliked doctors. Knew it was ridiculous when they'd effectively saved her life. But she'd been coddled for so long, eventually the rebellious teen moment had hit and they'd been a good target—better than hurting her family for simply loving her. But her brother and mother still hadn't seemed to have adjusted to her new status, even though the operation was a few years ago now. Same with everyone else she knew. Which was why she'd decided to move away and to keep moving.

'And boyfriends?'

She tightened the sheet about her. 'Not so good.'

'What happened?'

'I don't like everyone knowing.'

'And he told people.'

She nodded. 'And he was overprotective. *Really* overprotective.' Her sigh came from deep within. 'People change when they find out. I don't want this to be all that I am. Yes, it's part of me. But it's not all of me. I have more to offer than that. It's better if people don't know.'

'So what, you're going to stay covered up for ever?'

'Maybe.' She smiled. 'I'm going to start somewhere new again.'

'What if you fall in love and want to settle down?'

Settling down wasn't an option for her. Her own family had been to hell and back for her. She wasn't doing that to anyone else and she wasn't giving up her newly grasped freedom. She shrugged the question off. 'That's not on the horizon. I just want to live life now.'

'How do your family feel about your trip?' Unerringly he zeroed in on her weak spot—he seemed to have a real knack for that. She felt the blush. They didn't know the half of it. Thought she was in Australia for over a month and then heading straight to the UK. She hadn't told them about her detour on the way. Not wanting to worry them unnecessarily. She wasn't taking outrageous risks. She'd present it to them afterwards as a *fait accompli*—when her confidence was stronger. 'They're OK with it.'

Despicable. That was him. He should tell her. The truth. Now. But telling her would make her mad with him and he got the vibe she'd be less than impressed with his MD qualifications. Kind of ironic, seeing most women liked the idea of being with a doctor. Given they were usually rich and all. But Rhys was beyond rich too. And he liked the fact she didn't know either of those things about him. He liked the fact that she simply shared the raw physical attraction. It was basic. Why should they have to go any deeper than that? But already they were going deeper. Her words had an effect on him. 'Yes, it's part of me. But it's not all of me.' They had more in common than he was willing to admit. They'd both experienced trauma, defining them. She was determined to overcome hers. He could never leave his behind. Could never forget. Except when he was in her arms he felt better. Recharged. Couldn't he have that for just a little longer?

Rhys hadn't had such a selfish urge in a really, really long time. But, he reasoned, she need never know. They'd have this fantastic holiday fling together. Have a great time. He'd help her learn how wonderfully well her body worked. How desirable she was. Then she'd go and he'd head back to work refreshed and satisfied. Her company was invigorating. He hadn't had this much fun in what felt like for ever. He'd come back to life.

'Tell me about yours.'

He wondered what she meant for a moment. Then saw what she was looking at. His thigh. His scar. Memories flew at him. He wasn't ever rid of them for long. He never talked about it. Never would, with anyone.

'Skateboard accident.'

He heard it all. The squeal of the wheels as the brakes were slammed on—too late. The crunch of bone on concrete, the spattering sound of blood, the pulse weakening, the look in Theo's eyes as the life had literally bled out of him—the silent plea that Rhys had been unable to answer. If only he'd listened ten seconds before. If only he'd stopped when his kid cousin had asked. If only he hadn't been so hell-bent on being the fastest, the best...

He stopped the replay with the strength of mind that had got him through years of study, years of guilt.

He did not discuss the scar. Not with anyone.

He realised he'd been silent a while. She was watching him, watching whatever he'd let slip across his face. She looked serious and he knew she'd seen more than he'd intended. He flashed her a smile—charm mode. But the questions didn't leave her eyes. Her serious look intensified. Not buying it.

He needed a better method of distraction—for both her and him. He moved quickly, picked her up and carried her to the bathroom—the weight of her transforming the moment of angst to a moment of masculine pleasure. They just managed to fit in the shower.

She giggled at the ridiculously small cubicle. 'Practising for the Mile High Club, are we?'

'I think that'd be a piece of cake after this.' He hoisted her up against the wall. 'I like carrying you. Makes me feel all he-man.'

'And I'm the little woman? That is not a PC thing to say.'

He shrugged. 'What are you going to do? Sue me?' He scooped her higher so her breasts were almost at mouth height. 'Besides,' he added with unashamed arrogance, 'you like it.'

He kissed her body, let her slide down the wall so he could kiss her mouth. The pathetic trickle of water from the shower head was barely enough to wet her majestic hair. Man, he wished they were in his apartment. His bathroom was built for more than one occupant and had fantastic water pressure. He'd take the hose and spray the water all over her lithe limbs and then follow it with his hands and mouth. His appetite for her was huge and hardly filled.

She seemed to share the hunger for him. She swept her hands over his chest, traversing the indentations and ridges of muscle and bone.

'What do you do to keep fit?'

'Sail.'

On the few days he had away from work he'd spend hours on the water, in the water. Finding freedom with wind and sun and silence.

'You get muscles like these from sailing?' She started exploring them with her mouth as well as her fingers.

'It's not all just sitting around holding the tiller eating crab cakes.'

She mumbled as she kissed down his sternum. 'I've never been sailing.'

'We should go some time.' They should do everything.

'Would you take me below deck?'

She was heading south now and he could hardly answer. 'I'd take you above...below...in the cupboard where I keep the sails. You'd look sexy on my spinnaker.'

'Where do you sail?'

'On the...' *harbour.* He jerked out of the daze of desire.

He wasn't supposed to live in Sydney. What had he said— had he said? He'd thought Melbourne. Hell, he couldn't think at all when she did that. She didn't seem to have noticed his lack of answer. She was trailing her hands down his belly, watching as his body responded. Her eyes glazed, the flame in her face growing. He could think of nothing but her. 'What do you want?'

She didn't reply with words. Instead she made like him and let her actions speak—touching him with the hunger he had for her. She raised her head from where it had been deliciously close to where he really wanted her. 'Are you sore at all? From last night?'

Actually, yeah, his legs had been feeling it a bit today.

'Maybe you should lie down, let me do the work this time.'

He lost all ability to think, couldn't come up with a thing to say. She could be the boss. Fine. 'Uh, OK.'

They abandoned the shower, didn't bother with towels, just landed back on the bed in a hot, damp tangle. Her smile was so full of eager anticipation he had to close his eyes against the power of it. He lay on the bed and she knelt above him. Slowly roving over him from top to toe with her hands, her trailing hair, her hot mouth. Her roughened hands killing him with their firm grip and determined action. Exactly where he'd wanted her. Keeping control was such an effort—one certain to slice even more years off his life.

She guided him home. He gasped as she rode him hard. 'We're supposed to be pushing you, not me.'

She laughed, shook her head at him as she kept it crazy, fast, slow, faster again, keeping him on the edge until the heat was intolerable and his breath came harsh.

Sienna propped up her head by placing four of the thin pillows in the one pile, looked down her body to where he lay sprawled halfway down the bed. He'd spread her legs around him. Was seemingly having a wonderful time focusing on one at a time and exploring it—running smooth fingers down her thigh, twirling round her knee and back up again, fingers playing on her occasional freckles. She was almost reluctant to break into his enjoyment, but she couldn't resist talking to him, wanting to get to know him better. Wanting to break through his quiet charming façade and beyond into the vast reservoir that she sensed was there. There was a lot more going on with Rhys Monroe than he let show.

'You have such smooth hands. No calluses from hammering?'

He looked up, confusion flashing in his face.

She held up her hands to him. 'Look, hardly sexy, is it?' The calluses from hours and hours keeping the beat, from holding the drumsticks. Yet his palms were soft and smooth, surprising given he must spend hours and hours holding hammers and tools.

Dark shadows lurked in his eyes before the green light chased them away again. 'Actually, your hands are very sexy. You have a hold that is unique.'

'A hold?'

'Good friction.' He grinned wickedly.

'You like them?' She looked at the raised welts of toughened skin in amazement.

'There's nothing about your body I don't like.'

'How come you don't have workman's hands?' He didn't. He had the fine hands of a pianist. Long-fingered, smooth-skinned, neatly manicured.

He shrugged. 'I spend more time working inside than out these days.'

She was about to ask more but he diverted her, leaning over to follow the path of his deftly moving fingers with his mouth.

She couldn't concentrate on finding out about him, only what he was doing.

But he was learning about her—body and mind. His fingers probed while he posed questions. 'How come you ended up playing the drums?'

She leaned back on the pile of pillows, luxuriating in the wantonness of her position. Loving looking down and seeing his head nestled between her thighs. Delighting in the freedom to lie back and let him taste her as if she were the most delicious thing. 'I wanted to do something. I wasn't allowed to play sports. And I didn't have the puff for a wind instrument. I thought piano and strings were dull. I wanted to make the biggest, baddest noise I could.'

'Prove you were there, huh?'

She lifted her head to look at his expression. His astuteness was acute—and fascinating to her. He understood her so quickly and she had no hesitation in opening up further to him. Yes, she'd wanted to declare her existence to the world. Not wanting to have a mouse-like existence on the edge of life, hardly daring to move for fear her heart wouldn't cope with action. She'd wanted to claim her place, make enough noise to let others, and herself, know she was *there*. 'I like loud.'

'Do you, now?' His fingers climbed higher and his chuckle warmed her skin. 'I think I knew that.'

She giggled. He wiggled closer. Nuzzling the very top of her thigh.

'So why the holiday in Australia?'

'I wanted a week to relax before starting the big bit of my trip. Sydney has shopping, sun, surf…so long as I don't see any of your spiders and snakes I'm a happy tourist.'

He laughed. 'They don't tend to show themselves in the city much. You're in the clear, I think.'

'Maybe from the snakes but not the spiders. And they're

all poisonous, aren't they? I'm terrified every time I shower one will scuttle out of the drain.'

He nipped her tender skin, then licked it, soothing and seducing. 'Tell you what, I'll shower with you the rest of your holiday and scare them away.'

She grinned. 'OK.'

'And what's the big bit of your trip?'

She lay back, enjoying the delightfully slow way he was toying with her—the thin thread of desire being pulled ever tighter. 'Checking a few things off my list.'

'List?'

'Yeah, things I want to achieve before I die.'

His head jerked up. 'I thought you weren't about to die.'

'Well, hopefully not.' She gave him a reassuring grin. 'But it's time to take control of my life and do the things I've always thought I'd never be able to do.'

He looked at her for a long moment. 'Like what?'

'Silly things.' She felt her cheeks heat. She wasn't going to tell him he'd just helped her achieve something she'd never imagined would really be possible. 'I don't mean climb Everest or be the first person on Mars or win a Nobel Prize. I mean, play in a fountain on a sunny day type of things. Eat too many hotdogs at the fair.'

'That's not that silly.' He kept his eyes trained on her, his hands gently stroking up and down her inner thighs. 'You're not planning on doing dangerous things, are you? Like swimming with sharks, or walking on burning embers—in search of some extreme adrenalin rush? Prove your existence that way?'

'Hell, no.' She shuddered. 'It's not about risk. It's about knowing I'm alive and loving it, that I'm not taking life for granted. I want to live here and now, make the most of every moment.'

There was a long silence. She peeked down at him. Serious

and contemplative, he seemed miles away. He looked up and saw her watching him. 'Are you ready to make the most of this moment?' His hands slid back to the top of her thighs. Heat flooded her—ridiculous that she should feel any embarrassment now they'd been in this bed for so many hours, being as intimate as it was possible for two people to physically be. But this intimacy wasn't just physical. She was talking with a freedom she hadn't had before. He didn't judge, he simply listened and all the while made her feel sexier than hell. Killer combo. She'd never seen lust so raw like this. Never imagined a guy could even look this way—let alone at her. Never realised how intoxicating it was when she felt it in return—threefold.

Unable to stop, she tilted her hips up to him, silently issuing the invitation—access all areas.

She sprawled back on the flat mattress, having swept away all the pillows in her fight for release, a film of sweat on her brow. But he wasn't done. His gentle exploration, of both her body and life, began again.

'You have a job?'

'Not now. I worked all sorts to save for this trip—in bars, temping, gigs, session recordings.' She'd worked hard—not wanting to use her brother's money although he'd offered time and time again. She wanted to be free of his concern, his wellintentioned control. She wanted to do it all by herself. And while she had good grades and talent, right now she was factoring in the 'me-time'.

'You don't want to be a full-time musician?'

'Music is great but the lifestyle isn't.' And she wanted something more—to make a difference somewhere, somehow. Now she had a life she wanted to achieve something with it.

'Why not teach?'

She frowned.

He laughed. 'Come on, short work days, all those holidays…'

She threw him a sceptical look. 'Which shows how much you know about teaching.' It was a great profession but she'd have to do more study. She couldn't afford that time-wise or dollar-wise at present. Top of her agenda was travelling to the places she'd dreamed of for too long, then she'd work in the UK and decide. Ideally she'd like to work in a voluntary sector—helping out in areas where little help was usually available or affordable. But she still had to eat.

'So what are you going to do?'

Something important. Something useful. Something fulfilling. 'I don't know yet. Does it matter?'

'Yes—to you. That's what you're looking for, isn't it? A way to make your mark? Something positive.'

Too astute by half.

'You'd make a good teacher,' he persisted. 'Teachers are really important.'

'I know.' She sighed. 'You sound like my brother—actually he's a builder, or was. Now he's into commercial property development.'

'Great.'

A bland response if ever there was one. But Sienna wanted to hone in on some commonality—wanting something to link them besides the physical ache for each other. And he was so damn reticent when it came to talking about himself. 'You do residential property? People's houses?'

'Uh? Yeah.' He looked away from her, down her legs again. 'Tell me more about this list of yours. Is multiple orgasms on it?'

Rhys was still deep inside her, the overwhelming sensations still reverberating in his brain and body when she spoke.

'What about you? You have some things you want to do before you die?'

'I guess.' He could die now a happy man. No. Correction. He needed to experience her softness again. It registered that he wasn't going to be happy again until he'd had more of her. A lot more.

She'd said she wanted to live life in the moment—to make the most of it. He realised that he felt more alive when he was with her like this than he had done in years. She was more addictive than the most dangerous narcotic. The way she felt, the way she smelt, the sounds she made, the touch she gave. All combined to hit him with a natural high that he wanted again and again.

But it was just sex. He hadn't focused like this in a while, that was all. Hadn't lain in bed all night and half the day with a woman and done everything and anything on a whim.

But it wasn't quite just sex. She was interesting. He was interested in learning more about her—and not just her body. She had a refreshing outlook, a different drive from other people he knew. She wanted to make the most of every moment. He wanted a piece of her attitude for himself. 'I think we should trade.'

'Hmm?' She was drowsy, looking dazed and sleepy.

'Something I want to do. Something you want to do.' Hell, she wanted to frolic in a fountain. As if that'd be hard. But he could give her some challenges. He could set up some things she'd never forget. It seemed important she never forget because he had the discomforting feeling he'd never forget her. Never forget the moment he'd first laid eyes on her. Certainly never forget the moment his lips first got to touch hers. 'Deal?'

The blue in her eyes deepened. 'What kind of things?'

He shrugged. 'All kinds of things. Like on your list. Let's cross a few off this week.'

'You want to trade items on our life to-do lists?'

He was intrigued to see colour flood into her cheeks. 'Exactly.' He raised a brow at her blush. 'What do you say?'

'Oka-a-ay. But I'm a tad nervous about what might be on your list.'

He laughed. 'Nothing illegal, honey.'

CHAPTER EIGHT

SIENNA woke early and found her body ached all over—serious workout stiffness. Rhys hadn't been kidding when he'd suggested testing how much she was capable of. He'd pushed her to the edge and beyond.

A huge chunk of her loved the hedonism of it—her body revelling in the physical release. But inescapable thoughts niggled at her. There was a part of her searching for more. Wanting more from him.

A couple of times in the night he'd turned to her, saying nothing but taking her again with an almost desperate desire. As if he was seeking something from her, but she didn't know what it was. She wished he'd open up. She was used to listening to people, getting their stories out, but he was that guarded, didn't offer up a thing—not verbally. His actions told her. He drove inside her as if the physical satisfaction she gave pacified some other, deeper demon inside him.

She rolled over and watched him sleeping. His expression was relaxed, dark lashes curved on his cheek, his mouth soft and sensuous in repose. She was sure he had needs, certain he had hurts, but she couldn't figure them out—couldn't figure him out. She didn't know if she was going to have time to. But she was damn well going to try.

He opened his eyes, looked about with a fidgety air that signalled he wasn't quite a natural hedonist either. 'We need to get out of this room.' He threw back the sheet and slid from the bed. 'Come on, we'll come back and shower. Right now I've got something you've got to do at least once in life.'

She pulled on her skirt, then hunted for her tee—a crumpled mess half under the bed. With a grin Rhys handed her one of his shirts. The relaxed intimacy of his action made her gooey inside. She didn't bother with a bra, just slipped a couple of buttons through. Suddenly not concerned about covering the scar. It was early, there'd be no one about and Rhys had seen it all. The loose cotton was cool and wearing his clothing made her feel sexy. His sparkling expression hinted he liked it too.

'Let's go before I get a better idea.' He laughed and she felt freedom—to explore everything with him.

Barefoot, he led the way down the stairs. She watched, amused at his vitality and good humour. He grabbed a bag from the back of the reception counter—the light was on but for once it seemed Curtis wasn't home. They snuck out across the quiet street and onto the beach.

She followed him across the sand. 'What?'

'Beach volleyball.'

'Oh, no.'

'The tiny bikini is not mandatory.' He winked. 'Well, it would be if this was our own private beach—actually then we'd be having a naturist tournament. Sadly, it's not, and as you are is just fine.'

'Rhys, I really suck with balls.'

He froze. Shot her a look. Started to laugh.

Fire-engine-red, she laughed too.

'I have a feeling you'll do just fine. Anyway, it's early, no one's around to watch.'

Yeah, just you. It was all right for him. She watched the way he bent and pulled a ball from the bag. He had effortless grace, natural style.

He tossed the ball from one hand to the other, obviously amused by her reluctance. 'I thought you wanted to live now?'

She lunged for the ball as he threw it. 'You were one of those guys who could do any sport, weren't you? Rugby in the winter…'

'Cricket in the summer.' He laughed. 'Basketball, swimming, sailing.'

'And you were good all round.' She retrieved the ball from where it had rolled along the sand, lobbed it back.

'Excellent all round.'

She raised her brow.

He threw it back and spread his hands in mock humility. 'Well, that is the family motto.'

'You have a family motto?'

His humour dimmed and his grin became barely there. 'Do the best, be the best—excellence all round.'

'Wow.'

'We have a duty to perform.'

'A duty?'

'Sure. A responsibility.'

She dropped the ball. Again. It took less than three minutes for him to realise she hadn't been kidding about her lack of skill. Laughing, he resorted to even simpler passes. 'A little practice, you'll go far.'

He chuckled at her 'yeah right' expression and abandoned the game completely. He toyed with the ball as they walked along the edge of the water. She gazed across the blue to the high-rise buildings. Loving the vibrancy of the city. Bright-eyed, she turned back to him. 'I've thought of something for the list.'

'Yeah?'

'I want to walk over the Harbour Bridge. You done that?'

'Hundreds of times. And I've driven over it thousands.' Sydney Harbour Bridge—the world-famous landmark and fairly key to being able to move around the city.

She giggled. 'I mean climb it. You know, they put you in harnesses and you climb up the arches.'

Rhys stared back at her, his good mood sinking. Of all the places in the whole city, she wanted to go there? Too high profile. They took endless photos on that thing. Rightly so, it was a great experience, but he wasn't going to be caught in the company of a woman—especially one as beautiful as Sienna—and have the snaps sold. This was his holiday, his escape, his moment of fantasy out of his real life and he wanted to protect it. He wanted to have time with her—just her and him and no interference. No prying eyes. 'I have a better plan for today.'

'What's better than the view from up there? It's not too hot, it's not windy.'

'Yeah, but I have something that can only be done today. Right now, in fact. Let's go!'

She was giving him a funny look but he didn't care. Right now he was too busy thinking over what he was going to come up with list-wise that could be done without attracting too much attention. And the guilt was eating him up. But he'd spent most of his adult life swallowing back guilt—why was he gagging now? He was in serious trouble. The only way he could assuage it was to do the things to her that had her shaking in his arms, shaking in joy. If he kept her in a state of bliss, he'd be absolved.

'Come on.' He pulled her to him, planted a kiss. Got way-laid as usual—he couldn't ever have just one kiss from her. He pushed at the shirt she wore, running his fingers along her delicate bones, wanting to take it off completely. His desire for her was in no way diminishing. He finally pulled back, stared into her flushed face. 'We need to get moving.'

Back in the hostel they darted past Reception, nodding at Curtis who was looking strangely edgy. For a fleeting moment Rhys felt sorry the guy had to work so many hours. Sienna tripped into the little bathroom. He let her monopolise the shower for a few minutes while he scratched round for an action plan. Hell, he must be able to think of something. Then the sound of the water spraying clued him in. Waterfall. Fountain. There must be one somewhere in the city.

Sienna followed a pace behind Rhys as he headed to the train platform. He'd hustled her out of the bathroom and got them back out the door. Curtis on Reception had said hi as they passed again. She'd seen the speculation in his eye. The overly keen interest as he watched them depart. What did he care? Surely they weren't the first hostel inmates he'd seen get it together.

They got on a train, mixing in with a few commuters, shared a secret smile as they sat close on the seat. Enjoying the rocking motion. Sienna secretly enjoying a fantasy of being alone in the carriage with him, late at night, with no threat of other passengers arriving and—

'Ever had sex on a train?'

Apparently they were wired into the same fantasy. She shook her head and grinned at him, admitting with her eyes she'd been dreaming about that exact scenario.

He bent his head and kissed her. 'We'll add it to the list.'

The park was beautiful—surprisingly green. It smelt fresh but the humidity was on the rise again. They walked through, around one corner into an isolated spot—trees and bushes forming a natural canopy. Then she heard it, the gentle trickle of water. Behind a small railing was the most pathetic fountain she'd ever seen.

'We came to see this?'

His grin was slightly shamefaced. 'You're in Sydney at the height of summer. You can't go expecting amazing waterfalls and fountains. We have water restrictions.'

She leant at the railing, struck dumb by the idea that he thought this was better than climbing up the Sydney Harbour Bridge. 'A kid couldn't splash in that, let alone two full-grown adults.'

He stared at it. 'No.'

'And though the morning's warm already it's not quite hot enough.'

'No.' He turned her in his arms to face him. Kissed her gently.

She pulled back to look at him in reproach. 'You think a few kisses are going to turn this into the experience of a lifetime?'

He didn't appear remotely abashed, green twinkling in his eyes.

'You must rate yourself pretty high.'

'I'm sorry, Sienna.' He sighed then, and it was a sigh of genuine regret. 'I'm not myself around you.'

He pulled away, picked up her bag from where it sat beside them, neatly clipped it onto his own. She grinned as he did so, not really minding at all. Just liking spending time with him, getting to know him, feeling more relaxed and content than she ever had. It was nice walking with nothing on her shoulders, feeling the warmth of the breeze through her tee shirt. It used to annoy her no end when her brother insisted on carrying her bag or heavy things. But Rhys taking the burden didn't bother her at all. He wasn't doing it because he was worried for her. He was just being nice. Really he'd been nothing but nice to her from the moment they'd met. He offered nothing more. Expected nothing more. He'd been honest from the beginning. He wanted her. And when she was gone, it was done. She was the one who'd have to get over it. And as the moments passed there was even more of an 'it' to get over.

On impulse she turned to him. 'Thank you, Rhys.'

'What for?'

'Everything.' She smiled. He was so straight up. 'I can really trust you.'

His face hardened. The green sparkle faded behind the slate. 'Sienna.'

Her smile faltered. She was used to him closing over when she attempted to inquire into his life, but just then she hadn't asked anything and right now he had the most remote expression she'd ever seen on him. 'What is it?'

'There's something I have to tell you.'

For a second all her vital organs stopped. Something was wrong. 'Don't tell me you have a girlfriend.'

'No, I don't have a girlfriend.' He flashed a tight smile. 'Want to offer yourself for the part?'

'OK. But I'm only in town for another few days. And so are you.' *Don't start messing with the arrangement, Rhys.* Not when she was only just keeping it real for herself. His deathly serious look panicked her. She couldn't cope with serious. She had to get on.

'That's just it. I'm uh…'

'You're not married.' Sure she was right on that one. He wasn't able to open up even a little way, he'd never open up to marriage.

'No.'

'OK, so you're not married and you don't already have a girlfriend. Are you in trouble with the law?'

'No. I…' He sighed. 'Sienna, please, let me finish.'

She should. Hell, what was she doing? Here he was finally

trying to say something important and she was stalling him. Because, she realised, she didn't want to hear it. Didn't want this illusion shattered. And he was about to smash it—she could see it in his eyes.

He opened his mouth, drew in a deep breath.

And then they heard it. The ear-piercing scream. Startled, they stared into each other's eyes as if questioning whether the other had heard it. And then sound came again—shouts and cries. They both turned and ran. Around the hedge encircling the fountain, through the trees.

They came upon masses of people. A pile of them bunched near one of the swing sets. Wisps of conversation came to them—disjointed commands filtering through the crowd. 'She's bleeding…she could be concussed…someone phone an ambulance.'

'Excuse me. Make way, please. I'm a doctor.'

Sienna stopped. The crowd parted. Rhys walked through.

The next few seconds were like a series of still shots in her mind. All she heard was his voice—'I'm a doctor'—over and over. She pulled herself together, walked closer as the crowd dispersed, parents relieved to be able to deal with their own upset kids now there was someone taking charge.

She looked about twelve, had blood spilling from a gash on her head. Was flat on her back. One of her legs was bent at a hideous angle below her shin. Sienna shut her eyes a moment, knowing that she'd just caught a glimpse of snapped bone. She opened them again, focused on him.

Rhys was on his knees next to her, talking softly. 'What's your name, sweetie?'

She looked stricken. He pushed back her hair with the lightest brush of his fingers, compassion clear in his expression, gentle warmth in his smile.

'Katie.'

'Katie.' The child and the white-faced woman on the other side of her, presumably her mother, spoke simultaneously. Sienna understood. When he looked at anyone that way they'd talk. They'd trust—just as she had.

'Hi, Katie. My name is Dr Rhys Maitland, but you can call me Rhys, OK?' He was feeling over her body with deft hands. Sienna saw the way he was concentrating on other things while he chatted to her, saw the keen look in his eye. She recognised that look. Assessing. Evaluating. Deciding on his approach. When he got within range of her leg the child cried.

'OK, sugar. We're going to get you all fixed up, OK?'

He kept talking to her low and quiet. The low, quiet tones he'd used with her, but they were still audible across the grounds.

'My friends are going to come and pick us up in the ambulance. Have you ever been in an ambulance before?'

One of the remaining bystanders next to Sienna turned to her. 'He's a doctor?'

'Apparently so.' Sienna looked back at Rhys. His experience and skill were obvious to everyone.

'Is he good?'

'Rhys is good at everything he does.' Especially lying.

It couldn't have been much more than five minutes till the ambulance arrived, by which time Rhys clearly had everything under control. He even had the mother smiling, and the girl—weakly through her tears. Sienna clenched her teeth, holding back the grimace. The crew leapt out, bags in hand. One had a toy koala that she gave to the girl to cuddle. The kid buried her face in the soft fur.

The other officer grinned at Rhys. 'Hey, hero. Can't keep away from it, can you? Not even on your holidays.'

Aside from a slight wry twist to his lips you wouldn't have

thought Rhys had heard the comment. Instead he focused on introducing them to Katie, then talking through her condition.

Sienna watched as he rapped out information. Cool, calm, still polite but so in control. The ambulance officers quickly getting onto it.

Dr Rhys. Spouting medical jargon and utterly at home in a scene of chaos and carnage.

Clinical.

She'd known he'd held something back from her, but this brought home just how little she knew of him. Had anything in the last few days been real?

Yes. Her stupid heart cried bitterly. Those moments in his arms had been the most real thing she'd ever experienced.

But she pushed it away—sex. That was all it had been. Some stupid game. For whatever reason—and what the hell reason it could have been was utterly beyond her—he'd fabricated his entire life. And the thing was he'd done that right from the very beginning.

Why hadn't he told her? He'd lied. And at no point had he withdrawn from that lie. The only thing that appeared to be true was that he was on holiday—but from his job in *this* city, as a damn doctor. Tears of shock and hurt, wounded pride and wounded heart sprang in her eyes. He must have thought she was such a fool. Why, why, why? When she'd been so honest with him?

Rhys worked alongside Melissa and Simon to make Katie comfortable. Grateful it was a team from his own hospital. He'd figured it would be. They were in his catchment area. Hadn't allowed himself to even think of Sienna until now—needing to focus entirely on stabilising the situation. Needing to keep control of his own careering emotions. He always struggled when it was a younger patient. He always saw

Theo's eyes—the unmistakable plea for help, the light fading. This time he could help. This time it would be OK. But his heart still thundered and he kept the sweats at bay with a level of self-command that had taken some years to perfect.

He knew his control would be even more precarious if he stopped to think about what Sienna was making of it all. He'd been about to make a clean breast of it. Unable to hold back from her, wanting her to know the truth because he couldn't stand it any more, he had needed to fix it. It had been such a stupid idea in the first place—making up a new name, a different job—and yet, he couldn't wholly regret it.

But, damn, she'd just found out only half the truth in the most unfortunate way. He finally braved a glance her way. Saw her white face. Saw the furious hurt in her eyes.

He looked away again super quick. He wasn't free from his duty yet and until he was he couldn't work on Sienna.

He heard Melissa talking to the mother.

'Don't worry. She's in great hands.'

Rhys flashed a silencing look but Melissa was in full reassurance mode, taking the woman's arm and leading her to the open doors of the ambulance, her high tones carrying halfway across the park. 'Your daughter was lucky to have the city's best ER doctor on a walk in the park today. Dr Rhys is brilliant. She's going to be just fine.'

'OK, Melissa.' *Shut up.* 'Load up, we need to get to the hospital.'

'We can handle it from here if you want, Rhys. You don't need to come with us.'

'Of course I do. I need to clean up and do the paperwork anyway.'

He'd never leave a patient. He looked around again before stepping into the back of the ambulance. Wanting to at least offer a smile, call that he'd see her back at the hostel.

Knowing it wasn't enough, but better than nothing. He scanned the crowd.

She was already gone.

CHAPTER NINE

RHYS' hands itched. He hadn't got back to the hostel for hours—waylaid by people at the hospital who had seemed to think he'd fallen off the face of the earth because he hadn't been at work 24/7 as usual. Regardless that he was supposed to be having a holiday. They had seemed stunned that he actually had. Teased that he still couldn't keep away—not even a full week. If they'd only stopped talking to him he'd have been out of there a lot sooner. For once he hadn't wanted to be there a second longer than necessary.

There'd been no sign of Sienna when he'd got back to his room. Her stuff had vanished. She hadn't appeared the rest of the afternoon or evening. He'd patrolled the place, but hadn't dared enter the dorm room in the middle of the night— imagining all too well the scandalous headlines that might cause. So now, the next day, he was in for the sit and wait. He could hardly raise a polite response to Curtis' idle chat. But no way was he leaving Reception until he'd seen her. Desperate to explain. Determined to get her over that anger. Disproportionately upset that she was mad at him.

He sighed in frustration. Why should it matter? She was his holiday fling. She'd be out of here in just a few days. But it mattered an awful lot. How the hell could he make it right?

He'd been such a fool. He glanced at her day pack parked next to him on the sofa.

Anxiety ate at him. Where the hell was she? He didn't know if she was on meds. After an op like that a patient was usually on drugs long-term. Had she missed them? He unzipped the bag, needing to check.

A fabric-covered book was at the top. He knew what it was. He concentrated fiercely on his integrity. He'd been enough of a jerk. Not going to be tempted. Not going to pry into her personal thoughts. Much as part of him would love to. Purely to understand.

But as he lifted the journal to look underneath for any medicine packets, a piece of paper fluttered from it to the floor and as he picked it up his eyes automatically scanned it. Computed it. Sealed it in his brain. And acidic disappointment flooded his entire body.

It wasn't until after two p.m. that she appeared. Flanked by the inevitable army of girls from the hostel. She saw him as soon as she walked into Reception. Her eyes flashed and her cheeks flushed redder than they already were. She looked hot and bothered. Well, she wasn't nearly as bothered as him.

'Had a good day?' He managed to grate the words out, leaping to his feet and intercepting her.

'I don't think I'm talking to you. In fact, I don't think I even know your name—do I?'

'Rhys. My name is Rhys.'

'Rhys Monroe?'

'No.'

'And are you a builder, Rhys?'

'No.'

'Naughty, naughty Rhys,' Mistress South Africa said.

He ignored her. Held up the day pack in front of Sienna. 'Want this back?'

Her eyes flashed fire. 'Yes.'

'Then come with me now and I'll give it to you.'

'You can give it to me here.'

'No. I'll give it to you once we've sat down and talked about this like adults.'

'I really don't see that we have that much to say. You lied. End of story.'

He studied her. Wanting to throw his own accusations but conscious of the greedy interest of the others, conscious of how tired she looked. She seemed to have got thinner overnight. 'I'm walking out of here right now. If you want this back, you're coming with me.'

He wanted away from all the observers. He wanted just him and her again. He knew she'd come. Hell, if nothing else, he had her medication—and her passport.

She said nothing. Just turned and marched ahead of him. Waited on the footpath outside for him to point out the direction. Despite his own fury he couldn't stop the grudging smile inside. What would she do if he told her how beautiful she looked when she was mad?

Sienna sizzled all the way along the street. Fuming. She'd had an awful night's sleep, and an even more miserable day trying to take in some exciting tourist stuff, but all her mind would let her see was the sight of Rhys in full doctor mode. She replayed the moment of realisation over and over as she searched for reasons—consistently failing to figure answers.

That was why she was walking with him. She wanted answers and that was all she was after. She didn't want anything more from him now—right? Certainly not any more of his hot body.

Except that was all she could think about right this very second. How different he seemed. As gorgeous as the day before but now even more energy bounced off him. He exuded an aura of barely leashed passion. It had her on edge. It had her excited. In turn, that made her even madder.

He stopped a few yards along from the hostel.

'What's this?'

'My car.'

She stared at the shiny black convertible. 'Car? You brought your car on holiday with you? All the way from… where was it you said you were from again?' She raised her brows at him—attempting a look of cool inquisition but any *faux* haughtiness evaporated at his angry expression. How dared he look so cross when he was the one who'd fibbed his way through the last four days?

'We're not here to discuss my car, Sienna. Get in.'

Her mouth dropped. 'Ever heard of the word please?'

'Get in. Now.'

If he didn't have her most precious things in his hand, she'd walk away this instant. If he didn't have a hold on something even more precious of hers she'd be running like an Olympian. Then again, given he actually had all this precious stuff of hers, she should be flying.

Instead, she got in the passenger seat and slammed the door behind her.

He started the engine and drove. She had no idea where. But after half an hour of simmering silence he pulled into a park and got out of the car.

He walked ahead of her, brandishing her bag. She marched after him. Quite happy by now to give him one hell of a piece of her mind because he was really, really, asking for it.

He turned into a doorway. She blinked as she stepped out of the dazzling sunlight and into a gloomy interior. They were in a small bar. Guitar music played softly. Spanish. He led her to a table at the front, with booth seats ninety degrees to the window. He didn't sit, just gestured for her to and then, not bothering to wait for the waitress, went straight to the bar and ordered.

Sienna sat, studiously stared out the window, pretended she wasn't remotely interested in what he was doing.

Two cool beers in long glasses were plonked onto the table. He slid into the bench seat across from hers.

Much as she wanted to she couldn't refuse the drink—parched. She picked it up and drank deeply. He did the same. Half-empty glasses returned to the table with equally violent bangs.

'You lied to me.'

He sat back, seeming to relax a little. 'Yes.'

'You made up a name. You made up a whole story about yourself.'

'Yes.'

'And you think that's OK?'

'Of course not. But what about you? What about your *list?*' Scathing to say the least.

She sat up. 'What about it?'

'What about number *one* on your list?'

Blood pounded through every vein. 'You read my journal?' She watched, immobile and enraged, as with calm movements he unzipped her bag. 'Hand that over this instant. That is not your property. You have no right to read that.'

'I didn't. This page fell out when I opened your pack.'

'Why were you going through my pack?'

'I was worried. I wanted to see if you had any medication you'd missed.'

She stopped, jaw dropping; the world she saw was suddenly stained red. *Dr Rhys.* Interfering already.

'Anyway, so what if I read it? You wrote it to be read. That's why people write things down—so they get read.'

'Rubbish,' she snapped. 'Writing goals down helps make them real. Helps you realise them.'

'And that's what this was? Some *goal?*' He picked up the page and read in cutting tones. '"*1. To have wild, abandoned sex with someone who doesn't know about my heart condition.*"'

'And?' With superwoman strength she hid the cringe. OK, it sounded trashy read aloud, but so what? What business was it of his? It was a fantasy, for heaven's sake. One she'd never imagined would ever actually happen.

'So *anyone* would have done? You just wanted the experience of being with someone who didn't know about you. Well, lucky me. Right place, right time. Good thing I got to the table when I did or would you have gone for Tim, or Gaz or some other sucker on the dance floor? Anyone so long as it was dark and he could satisfy you?'

Incensed, she threw it back on him. 'Well, as I remember it you weren't exactly complaining. Don't make out like I've used you any more than you've used me.' She choked the words out. 'Don't you dare come across all holier than thou. It's not like you were out looking for a serious relationship either. Were you? You can't even tell me your real name. For days you've been lying to me. I was up front a hell of a lot sooner than you.' And, no, of course she wouldn't have gone for Tim or Gaz or anyone else in the whole entire world. Because she'd never felt that instant, unstoppable attraction to another before. Not that she was about to tell him that. How dared he judge her? 'It was a one-night stand. That was all either of us intended.'

'How do you know?'

Astounded, she stared. 'How can you say that? We'd known each other thirty seconds before we had sex. Conversed on nothings for a minute max. Relationships don't start that way, Rhys. And we're certainly missing out on the fundamentals of any kind of relationship—like honesty, like trust.' Utterly defensive, she stormed at him. Of course it had meant more and secretly hadn't she dreamed? Stupidly. But now she was out to salvage what little pride she had left. She'd downplay it—how it had felt and what it had meant— because he hadn't even been honest with her about his name.

Besides, she needed to protect herself. Serious relationships weren't for her, remember? She couldn't offer happy ever after to anyone. She might not have the ever and after.

He jerked, sitting bolt upright, glaring at her, looking as if he was about to launch a blistering attack. His eyes glowed green but his jaw clamped. For a long moment he sat rigid. Finally, vehemently, he threw her words back at her. 'What we did wasn't sleazy.'

She met his gaze then, held it for a moment, and then they both looked to the glasses on the table.

'OK.' He spoke more softly. 'So neither of us has been entirely honest.'

She looked back at him, anger refuelled. 'I might have had secrets but I have been honest. You're the one who hasn't. Why lie? What have you got to hide?' She gave a mocking laugh. 'Do tell me, who are you really, Rhys?'

'Here are your tapas, Rhys.' The waitress stood with a tray covered in tiny dishes, her glance flicking between the two of them—her attempt to maintain a bland expression a complete failure.

Sienna turned to the woman. 'What's his surname?'

'I'm sorry?'

'His surname. What is it?'

'Sienna.'

'Maitland,' the waitress replied just as Rhys interjected.

Sienna sat back in the seat and stared at him through narrowed eyes.

'Thanks, Tracey, that's fine.' Rhys smiled at the waitress, who was looking at Sienna as if she were some crazy lady. She'd set the dishes across the table and given them a plate each and after Rhys' words she turned and practically ran to the bar where the other waitress was lounging, watching.

Rhys stared back at Sienna. Eyes hard, the glow gone. 'Eat. You need it.'

She needed answers more. 'Who are you and why did you lie to me?'

'Stuff some chorizo into your mouth and I'll answer. Maybe then I'll have a chance of finishing before you interrupt me.'

Mutinously she picked up the fork and stabbed the sausage several times. His lips twitched.

He picked up an olive and, ignoring his own etiquette advice, put it in his mouth and talked at the same time. 'My name is Rhys Maitland and I'm a doctor. I work in the ER department of the hospital down the road and I've lived in Sydney all my life.'

She swallowed. 'Why didn't you tell me that at the start?'

Rhys thought about his response. No matter how he framed this he was going to come across as a jerk. Then again, that might be an improvement on her current perception of him. 'I just wanted to escape.'

'What on earth have you got to escape from?'

He decided to give her the easy answer—the only answer he'd be able to tell anyone. 'I'm the heir of a multi-million sportswear empire.'

'What?'

'I'm worth millions. I have a trust fund I inherited from my grandfather and I'll inherit most of the company shares from my father. My family is…well-known in Sydney. We're in the society pages, my cousin's wedding was in the weekly women's magazines, that sort of thing.'

She looked blank. 'Are you telling me you're some sort of celebrity, Rhys?'

'Not by choice. No, not really.' He sighed. 'A little. I try to avoid that rubbish. But sometimes, there are events I have to go to, and the press are there and because of the money, the name, they write about it.' Like the eligible bachelors spread some rag had done a couple of months ago that had made life a living hell at the hospital for some time.

'So you have all this money but you work as a doctor.'

He nodded, could see the thought processes. The next question was obvious.

'Why?'

'Why what?' He stalled. He knew where she was going and he didn't want to answer. Some things you could never escape from.

'Why medicine? Why not the family business?'

'I wanted to do something useful.' Instantly he saw more questions leap in her mind but he headed her off. 'Anyway, back to why I lied. I get sick of people only being interested in me because of my bank balance. I wanted to be away from me, from the preconceived ideas people have. I think that's something you can understand, isn't it?' He looked at her pointedly.

He'd got away all right. He'd been acting in a manner totally unlike himself—acting crazy. It wasn't just about her not knowing who he was; it was about him being free to do whatever he fancied. And he fancied her. He continued the confession. 'I am on holiday this week. Tim works at the hospital with me and is in his band for fun. I went along to help with the gear for the gig. Met you. Knew you weren't from town—' He broke off. Realising he was heading into mud the way he was telling it.

'So *I* was the lucky one,' she carried on for him softly. 'Right place, right time. Right tourist.'

Not true. He'd never behaved like that in his life. Never wanted someone the way he'd wanted her—in the very instant he saw her. It was as if she'd switched the on button to his main power source. Until now he'd been functioning at fifty per cent. But he wasn't about to tell her that. Not when she was wearing a frown that would rival Attila the Hun's. Not when he was still irrationally angry with her. It bothered him beyond belief. The idea that she'd just wanted to have sex with someone—anyone—who was ignorant of her history, was utterly galling. He wanted to be more than that. This *mattered,* and he wanted it to matter to her too. He couldn't hold back the bitterness in his tone. 'I guess we're even.'

Her hand wobbled out to her glass. Despite the food she looked pale, unhappy and beautiful. His anger evaporated in the warmth of concern and the heat of desire. He wanted to get out of here, wanted to take her to his apartment so they could lie down—rest and relax. He wanted his holiday to come home. Wanted to see her there. Definitely wanted her in the bathroom.

But the strain in her eyes slowed his libido down. She'd argue it till she was blue in the face but the fact was she was vulnerable. She did have to take extra care. There were higher risks for her—a trip to the dentist could cause her problems.

Rhys shifted on his seat. He didn't have room in his heart for her kind of vulnerable. He couldn't afford to get too involved. He had to protect his bruised heart as much as she literally had to protect hers.

'Have something more to eat.' He took her wrist in his hand as he spoke. Surreptitiously keen to read her pulse, but initially thrown by the erratic beat of his own heart, he held on that little too long.

'Why are you holding my wrist like this?' She stared at his fingers. 'Are you taking my pulse? You jerk. How dare you?'

He felt the beat quicken even before her words were all out her mouth. 'You look like hell.'

'Any wonder? And you've been doing the overprotective bit this whole time, haven't you?'

'What? Don't you accuse me of mollycoddling you or treating you any different from how I'd treat anyone.'

'That's just the point though, isn't it, Rhys? You're a doctor. You *treat* people.'

He lowered his voice. 'You know exactly how far I've pushed you—the extremes I've pushed you to.' And himself. If he was honest, he was going beyond his comfort zone even now. But he couldn't seem to stop. He wanted to make things right with her.

But she was off on a bender. 'This is why you stopped me from doing the bridge walk. You've been protecting me?'

'No.'

Sienna laughed harshly. 'You really are incredible, you know that, Rhys? You thought I couldn't do it, didn't you? That I couldn't even manage some stairs?'

'That is not why I didn't want to do the bridge walk, Sienna.' He breathed out heavily. Damn the woman and her incessant interrogation. He wanted to be honest but still felt the usual constraint about telling her anything. The last thing he wanted to do was relive the Mandy experience. And he didn't want to put ideas into her head—about selling her story. But at the same time he wanted to straighten this mess out. Reluctance swamped him but the need to resolve things with her won over his reservations about inviting her into his world. 'It's complicated.'

'Is everything complicated with you?'

'No more than it is with you.'

'I'm not that complicated, Rhys.'

'That's not true, Sienna. There are depths in you. Areas you don't let anyone into.'

* * *

Sienna looked across the table at him. She might have a few dark corners, but his no-go areas were vast fields. 'That's true of anyone.' She picked up an olive. 'Anything you told me in the last few days—the sailing, the family motto. Was any of it true?'

'Every word.'

She paused, the olive halfway to her mouth. She really wanted not to believe him. But the intensity in his answer was compelling. She could feel him willing her to see him as genuine.

'Can't we just forget about all this rubbish? You know me, Sienna. I know you. I want to keep challenging you.'

She sat back. He was all challenge. He was the challenge of her life. And she couldn't walk away. 'I don't think I know you at all, Rhys.'

'Look. Come back to my apartment with me now. Let me show you.'

She shifted on the seat. Not sure what he meant by 'show'— not sure how she felt about letting him in again that way.

He read her mind. 'I'll run you back to the hostel any time you want—you just say the word.'

CHAPTER TEN

IT WAS a two-minute walk to his apartment. They swept past the security guard who managed to keep his curiosity marginally better hidden than the waitress had. They got in the lift. Rhys pressed several buttons on the keypad and then the lift ascended.

There was another keypad outside his apartment door. Another series of buttons were punched. He looked up and caught Sienna's look of surprise. 'I value my privacy.'

'I could never remember a code that long.'

Once inside she looked around his apartment. He hadn't been kidding about the money thing. Her brother was rich, but this was on a whole other level. The fittings, the furniture, the air, the art—it all screamed extreme amounts of money mixed with good taste.

He watched as she took it all in. 'Does it make a difference?'

'Not to me,' she answered, irritated that he'd think it would. 'Why? You think I'm going to ask you to pay me?'

'No!' he snapped.

His flare irritated her more. 'Then don't insult me. The only person this makes a difference to is you.'

'You're probably right.' A hint of apology crossed his expression as he stood in the centre of the room. 'So this is me.' He gestured wide, a little self-consciously.

She looked at him, rather than his home. She knew some things now, more made sense. But she also knew he had stuff still buried deep that he chose to ignore. It was in his eyes, the mirror reflecting his reticence. His dislike of the media and attention might answer some of it, but there was more to it and she, like the proverbial cat, was curious. That, together with concern, motivated her decision to be here.

Now that he'd invited her here he seemed a little at a loss to know what to do with her. She helped him out. 'You going to make me a coffee?'

He moved then, reminded of his host duties. 'You don't want wine?'

She shook her head. The beer she'd had at the bar had been enough. She needed to keep her wits about her and her will firm. Already she was in danger of forgiving all and letting him get away with anything. There was something so irresistible about his strength and silence and in the occasional vulnerability she saw in his full, sensual mouth. Part of her was so tempted to make a move—this was merely a holiday fling, after all. But she was deluding herself and she knew it. So instead she'd give them a moment for closure and then go back to the hostel. If she stayed around him she'd slip further under his spell and that would be stupid. Falling in love wasn't an option—marriage, kids and a white picket fence were off the list. For the well-being of everyone.

Aside from the art and the opulence there was little to distinguish his apartment from any other bachelor pad. Overflowing bookcases, a state-of-the-art entertainment system that included games console, stereo, masses of CDs and DVDs.

She followed him into the kitchen area and as she turned to admire the gleaming espresso machine she saw what hung on the dividing wall.

It was covered with black and white photos printed on

canvas blocks. Varying sizes. Varying groupings. Formal portraits, family snaps. All had been digitally enhanced, then printed onto the canvas. Occasional stripes of colour had been painted on, or tiny details filled in. Some photos were left plain, others had been added to. The effect as a whole was striking—a dramatically different sort of 'rogues' gallery'.

Sienna stared and stared. Finally asked, 'Family?'

He nodded. Eventually gave some more detail. 'My sister did it for me. She's a photographic artist. She does some interesting stuff.'

'This is really cool.' She walked closer, wanting to see if she could guess. She pointed to one shot of a young couple in older style wedding clothes. 'Your parents?'

He nodded, slowly coming to stand beside her.

She pointed to a roly-poly baby. 'You?'

Again a jerky affirmative.

There was a shot to the side of two wide-smiling boys aged maybe eight and ten, the elder one clearly Rhys. 'Your brother?'

He walked, angled away from her, arms folded across the front of his body. She could see his hands were curled into fists. 'Cousin.'

She stared at him. His 'conversation closed' body language couldn't be any louder. She glanced again at the picture then moved on. 'Which is your sister?'

He came back. Obviously reluctant. Pointed, but immediately pulled his head back so his arms became bars across his chest.

'She's younger?'

He nodded.

She smiled. 'Are you a bossy, overprotective older brother?'

'She'd probably say so. I'd say I'm the responsible one.'

'Responsible.' Not the first time that had come up. She turned to him. 'It's a balance, isn't it? Yes, you have to be responsible but you also have to *live*. And let others live their lives too.'

'Yes, but you also have to recognise you have responsibilities to others—especially those you care about and who care about you.'

Sienna knew that. It was precisely why she didn't want someone getting too close. She didn't want to be stifled. And, ultimately, she didn't want to let them down.

Rhys stared back at the wall. 'You also have a duty to help where you can. A duty not to hurt, not to let people down.' As his last words echoed her thoughts, his gaze landed on the picture of him with his cousin.

Sienna was hit by a horrible thought. 'Is that why you came after me? After I showed you my scar—you felt a duty?'

'Not a duty. No.'

'No? You didn't feel bound not to leave me feeling bad?'

'No.' He turned away from the pictures and faced her. 'I came after you because I couldn't not.'

'So it was a duty.'

His gaze locked with hers. 'It was desire. It's still desire.' He stepped closer, his reserve breaking. 'I like how I feel when I'm around you.' He put his hands on her shoulders, his fingers firm. 'I like how I feel when I touch you.' He drew closer still, speaking quietly yet every word rang loud. 'I can't help but want to touch you.'

He kissed her then, a soft brush that had her parting and wanting. So much for closure.

He looked down at her, his lips a fraction from hers, his eyes burning bright. 'You have no idea how much I want to make love to you.'

Her gasp was soft and in that very instant his mouth was back on hers, preventing her response, stopping her from voicing her doubt. Sending that doubt packing.

They kissed and kissed and kissed again. A couple of times he pulled away from her lips, kissing down her throat but as quickly he was back to her mouth as if unable to keep away, as if needing to taste the sweet intimacy.

Her resistance melted in the onslaught. As his hands framed her face, cradling her as he kissed her so tenderly, a wave of emotion rose in her and was more than enough to drown her hesitation and hurt. She closed her eyes and absorbed the care he was taking. She was too overwhelmed by sensation to realise he'd been slowly walking them somewhere. Not once breaking the kiss, not giving her the chance to take breath and reclaim sanity, he guided her to his room. With desire-drugged eyes she took in vague details. Just a glimpse of the bed had her knees pathetically weakening.

'I'm sorry I lied.' And she knew that he was. And she wanted to forgive him. She did. But he was still holding a part of himself back, and she knew it and she couldn't quite say it didn't matter.

'Rhys…' She should go back to the hostel. She shouldn't let this become anything more. But the change was already happening; she could feel it swirling around her.

'Let me show you.' He made it so utterly impossible to say no.

He gently set about removing her clothes. She raised her arms so he could slide the tee shirt off her, stepped out of the skirt as it puddled around her feet. Naked for him again, baring everything. Could he do the same for her?

Her senses flared as he stripped. The way he touched her, the way he looked at her, she almost couldn't bear it. His tenderness was so intense she felt more bowled over than if he'd bodily picked her up and taken her barbarian-style on the bed. Instead he moved with deliberate leisure over the length of her body, proving a level of passion that she could scarcely believe. She'd been treated gingerly before. This was different. This was genuine—it felt like love.

She tasted his groan as he slowly pushed into her. She twisted her fingers in the hair at the back of his head, letting her other hand slide down the strong muscles of his back as gently, so gently, he moved against her. The press of his pelvis, the lock of his lips on hers, so they were joined and it was so deep, so complete. With arms wound tight about each other, nothing could come between them.

The simplest intimacy. So sublime.

Her head was spinning and the tears started falling before she was even aware of them until finally she had to break the kiss, arching her neck so she could gulp in one last breath before her body shuddered and her mind shattered.

'That's my girl.' His smile was tender and tight.

She stared up at him as she rode to the end of the crest, just as he hit his. Unwavering, fearless, their concentration sealed on each other as their bodies were.

Then there was silence. Stillness. She reminded herself to breathe. She'd just seen into his soul. And knew he'd seen hers.

Fear struck almost immediately. Rhys had good armour in place. Could she really believe in what she thought had been evident in his eyes? Some time soon she needed him to talk. She needed words as well as actions.

Right now she just needed to recover.

He lifted up from her, wiped away the tears on her cheek with the pad of his thumb. 'You OK?'

She nodded. Not wanting to risk a squeaky sob of a reply.

He lay on his side, pulled her hips so she too turned onto her side, her back to him. He snuggled close behind her, his arm heavy across her waist, his hand pressing against her chest. Relief flooded her—so glad she couldn't see him because she needed the respite. She felt raw and vulnerable, shaking with emotion so exquisite it almost hurt. This had been completely different from the wild abandonment that first night—the moment she'd thought could never be surpassed. She'd been wrong. Nothing could compare to what had just passed between them. And it frightened her more than anything had ever frightened her in her life. It wasn't supposed to have happened like this. Everything had changed.

He could feel her trembling still. He wondered if she could feel the tremors racking him too. He masked it by smoothing his hand down her back, wanting to soothe her. He regulated his breathing in time to the sweep of his hand.

He'd never felt like this. Never felt anything like that. What they had just shared was beyond comprehension. He hadn't been able to think of a single pyrotechnic thing, no technique, no position that would make all the fireworks in China explode in the one hit. He'd just wanted to worship her. To show her how sorry he was. How much he liked her. To treat her as she should be treated—precious, cherished, loved. And so he had. With gentle hands, soft touches, starting at the bottom, slowly he'd savoured his way up the length of her, sliding his hands up her slender calves and to the rest of her beauty. But it was when he'd finally drawn over her and slowly pushed deep inside her that he'd felt it. The world had stood still. And, for one moment, had been perfect.

How was it that this kept on getting better? That first time, in the cold store of the bar, had been crazy—wild and crazy and he'd never thought he'd feel such intensity again. But he had—time and time again with her. Fast, slow, risky or relaxed, it didn't matter, it just got better and better. A woman he barely knew. A woman he didn't know if he could trust. A woman who was vulnerable and whose vulnerability threatened him in his weakest spot. He couldn't be falling for her. Cardio thoracic surgeon he wasn't, but he knew enough. The likelihood of her needing more treatment in the future was pretty high, and he couldn't, wouldn't sit there and do nothing. Only able to watch while someone he loved...

Oh, God, he was in trouble.

Sienna knew it was the middle of the night but she couldn't sleep any more. Her brain had clicked on and was whirring at triple overtime rate. She listened to his regular breathing. She needed some space. Carefully she slid out from under his arm, slipped into the shirt on the floor and padded barefoot out to the lounge. She flipped the switch and quickly dimmed the light. Her bag was at the end of the sofa. She curled into the chair and opened the book. How to make sense of this? The blank page mocked her swirling, chaotic thoughts and emotions. Fear held the words back. Maybe she shouldn't overanalyse. Maybe she shouldn't even try to make sense of what was happening, of the secret desires rising in her. All the things she couldn't, shouldn't have.

Frustrated, she looked about the room. *Write anything to break through it. Describe the damn curtains.* And so she did. Putting order into her mind by describing the room she sat in. Ignoring the important things—like whose room it was and what she was doing in it wrapped in one of his shirts and nothing else. Trying to block out the melancholy that came when bliss was followed by uncertainty.

He'd said he wanted to make love to her, called her his girl. But these were just words—the soft nothings of pillow talk. This was the man who still couldn't seem to talk. Who was still so reticent and guarded—despite having invited her into his personal domain. Why didn't he trust her? What had happened that made him stay so locked up? She longed to break through to him. She knew she shouldn't, she was getting too involved, but how she wanted to. You always wanted what you couldn't have.

* * *

In his dream her belly was gently rounded. She put a hand to it, her secret smile teasing him. Then her belly was swollen tight and she sat naked, her breasts full, nipples darkening with maternal maturity. His body tensed with longing. His child. His family. Indescribable satisfaction surged through him.

But in that flash the picture fled. Suddenly it was images of the hospital speeding through his brain—medications and operations and tubes and beeps. And then it wasn't Sienna on the table, but a kid.

He snapped back. *No. No. No!* The sound of his own voice jerked Rhys awake. He took a couple of deep breaths. Pressed his hands to his eyes, keeping them closed. Not real. The sweat rapidly cooled, leaving him chilled. He tried to rationalise.

Rhys the clinician knew if ever she was pregnant it could be managed. Yes, there were higher risks, but nothing that medication and good care couldn't handle. And, yes, there was the chance that a heart condition might be passed on to her child. The chance was small but it was there.

Rhys the man couldn't handle even the smallest risk. Rhys didn't want to sit uselessly and suffer while his loved ones suffered.

Suddenly his arms ached with emptiness. He reached out to touch her, sat up sharply as his hand encountered the cold, empty sheet. The loss stabbed. How could he give to her if one day he woke to find her gone?

His heart thumped a wild tattoo. Then he saw the faint light coming through the hall. He slipped from the bed and pulled on boxers. Quietly he moved, unable to stop suspicion rising. She was huddled in his favourite chair, her head bent, scribbling in her journal. What details was she recording?

He stood in the shadow. Uncomfortable—with what had happened, with the crazy way his mind was messing with him, with what she was doing. How little he knew of her. Was she another Mandy? Was she transcribing their every word so she could sell it on? Rhys needed privacy. He needed to keep those deepest and darkest desires and secrets well hidden so he could keep their impact under control. But he'd just slipped up. He'd wanted to make up for his lie, but he'd given far more of himself than he'd intended. She'd slipped under his barriers. Had she known? He needed to back-pedal. Needed to get this back to the casual fling it had started as.

'What are you writing?'

She looked up and guilt flashed all over her face. 'Nothing.'

He hesitated. He could hardly demand to read it. He had to go on trust. He wasn't so good with that. 'You should be in bed.'

Get her back in bed, where he could keep an eye on her. She'd admitted she hadn't intended anything serious from this affair. He needed to think the same. Put it in the physical box and keep it there. No more questions, no more depth. No thoughts to a future that could leave him wide open to a level of pain he knew he couldn't handle.

She should be in bed? What was his angle—because he wanted her or because he was concerned for her? The last thing Sienna needed was another doctor. Scenes from the tapas bar tumbled back—the way he'd wanted her to eat, the way he'd tried to take her pulse, the fact he'd gone through her bag to find her medication. He couldn't help himself. Being a doctor was as much a part of him as his legs were. If this continued into a relationship he'd be mollycoddling her as badly as Neil had. She should walk. Go back to the hostel. Stop before the disappointment hit—inevitable as it was.

But his attraction was irresistible. He had such strength. She wanted to borrow some. And she also wanted to break through it, to whatever it was he was so fiercely protecting. She only had another couple of days in Sydney anyway. Live *now*.

But as he flopped back onto the bed and pulled her onto him, she wished for the carefree romp they'd enjoyed at the hostel. This was getting heavy, he was starting to matter too much and he was so far wrong for her. But while the joy he brought was so unimaginable, so indescribable, she just couldn't say no.

They spent most of the next morning lazing, testing each other's general knowledge by reading the questions from a trivia board game. Not bothering with the actual rules. Conversation stayed safe and simple. They shared favourite movies, favourite songs, most embarrassing moments. He joked, teased and laughed. She joked, teased and laughed. And all the while she knew she was finally getting the truth from him, but still not getting to the heart of him. The scar was key. She saw the way he sometimes rubbed at it. The way he avoided any mention of it.

She thought of her airport trek tomorrow. Hell, her backpack was still at the hostel, padlocked shut but still vulnerable under her bunk in the dorm room. While Rhys was in the bedroom she found the phone and called Curtis on Reception. Got him to put it in the secure room for her. Fobbed off his attempt at chit-chat and enquiries as to what she was up to.

'Who were you talking to?'

She spun, surprised at the accusatory tone in Rhys' voice.

'The hostel. I just got Curtis to lock my pack away for me.'

'Oh.' He walked across the room, tightened the blinds, keeping them wide enough for light to come in but for the world outside to be blurry.

Sienna couldn't stand it any more. Skirting around issues wasn't something she was good at. She was good at getting people to talk, and she wasn't going to have Rhys, someone who actually mattered, be her only failure.

She even had a plan. His bathroom was magnificent and already they'd spent quite some time investigating how much hot water was in the cylinder—lazing for hours under the shower. So in the late afternoon she suggested they return there. This time when she went in she eyed the double basins and twin towel racks with mock disfavour. 'You entertain here often?'

'No.' He grinned. 'I told you I like my privacy. I don't tend to have people over much.'

'I'm honoured.'

He laughed. 'You are not.'

'No, I am, Rhys. You letting me in here.' She shot him a not-so-innocent look from under her lashes. 'You must trust me.'

His smile remained on his mouth but his eyes went wary. 'Maybe a little.'

'How much?' She walked towards him. 'How much do you trust me?'

The wary look spread. He knew she wasn't joking around. 'Why, what do you want to do?'

'Not me, Rhys. You.'

'What do you want me to do?'

It was so easy, yet he seemed to find it so hard. 'Talk.'

He looked nonplussed. 'What about?'

'How you're feeling.'

'Oh, my God.' He looked at her as if she'd grown two heads. She laughed. 'It's not that bad. How about this? I touch you, and you tell me how it feels.'

'Touch?' His brows were up, she could tell he could cope with the touch bit. But he didn't know where she planned to lay her hands yet. 'OK.'

'Great. Let's start simple.' She cocked her head on the side and studied him. 'Where to begin… How about if I touch you here? How does that feel?' She ran her fingertips along the breadth of his shoulders.

'Not bad.'

'What about here?' She slid them down to his nipples, circled around them.

'Getting better.'

She went a little lower, crossing abs that went taut at her touch.

'Mmm hmm.'

'Words, Rhys, use your words.'

He grunted. 'You've got to be kidding me.'

She felt a touch of guilty amusement at his expression— half of him wanting her, half of him wanting her to shut up. She paused the downward trajectory of her fingertips and looked up to him, waiting.

The wanting half of him won. 'Isn't it obvious?'

She stayed silent.

He sighed. 'Would it make this simpler if I told you that anywhere you touch me feels good?'

'Well, now, that was a sweet thing to say.'

She squeezed some shower gel onto her hands, rubbed them together in circles to lather it up into a silky, bubbly mass. She skipped over the middle of him entirely. Dropped to her knees. She heard him suck in a quick breath.

She smiled up at him as she knelt before him.

'OK, I'm quite liking this.' He looked back down at her, cheeky grin on the full lips.

Yes, but he didn't know what she had planned. She spread her soapy hands and placed them on the front of his thighs, ran them down over his knees. Switched both hands to one leg and wrapped around his calf, sliding down with sensual slowness and back up.

He'd gone quiet again. She'd known he would. She gave

the other leg the same treatment, loving the spray of the water from the multiple shower jets warming her. This was way better than standing in some freezing fountain.

With nervous fingers she went back up his thigh with both hands. Slipped to the side and gently touched his scar. With light fingers she went back over it.

She sensed the change instantly. His tension was palpable, his body rigid. Silence. Even his breathing held in check. She brushed her lips against the puckered skin. Swept across it with a soft, open mouth.

He jerked away. 'Don't, Sienna.'

She ran soothing hands down his legs. 'Does it hurt?'

'No.' Brief.

She touched the scar again. His fists curled at his sides.

She knew he wanted her. But she sensed his anger as well. As sure as steam rose, it was rising, nearing the surface. He had such a seemingly impregnable veneer—quietly charming. But he used it to keep everyone at bay, granting no opening to his true emotion. She wanted to shatter it. Pierce through the layer to the passion and pain she knew simmered deep, deep below. So she traced over the scarred skin once more, first with a quick finger, then with lips, then with the tip of her tongue.

She heard him suck in a breath, struggle to rein in his temper.

'Sienna—'

She couldn't ignore the warning. She stood, laid a tender palm on his chest. Felt the strong, regular beat of his heart beneath. 'Does it hurt here, Rhys?'

Tension hung in the room. His face was like a mask. She let her fingers brush the scar again.

He jerked. 'Back off.'

She stepped after him. 'No.'

His arms crossed his chest. He took another step away. She walked forward another pace, and another half. Until his back was against the bathroom wall.

'Tell me.'

He stared down, eyes heavy-lidded. Almost shut. 'There's nothing to tell.'

She put her hands on his chest. 'Talk to me. Your challenge this time, Rhys. Talk to me.'

'Damn it, don't you know when to leave it alone?'

He moved fast. Spinning around, spinning her around so it was her turn to be pinned against the wall. His body slammed up hard against hers. The tiles were cold on her back. His thighs were hot between her own.

'I don't. Want. To talk.'

'Fine!' she yelled. Right in his face. 'Don't. Don't say a damn thing. Keep your secrets. Don't let anyone in. Don't let anyone get anywhere near you!'

'Near me? How near me do you want to get?' His hands went to her hips, pulling her hard against his. 'This near?' He jerked her closer so his erection dug hard against her lower belly. 'This?'

She rose on tiptoe, wrapped one leg around his waist so he couldn't step away. 'Closer.'

He kissed her then, hard and angry. She was angry too but it was whisked away when she sensed the hurt he was trying to hide. So she opened for him, and he took. Boy, did he take. The ferocity of his passion literally made her weak. It was as if the stronger he was, the softer she became. Her legs were no longer able to support her—gut instinct demanded she lie down and welcome. They slid to the floor, swiftly he moved, entering with a hard thrust and a harsh growl. Any pretence at foreplay was forgotten. She pulled him even closer. Pushed him further.

The water sprayed down on them and as she gazed up at

him it was like being under that fountain of her dreams. He could make her feel so wonderful, could make her feel as if she wanted to share everything with him. Most of all she wanted him to share with her. But this was only his body. She understood what he was seeking. The relief, the release, the joy that would obliterate the angst—momentarily. He wanted this to make him feel better. Why couldn't he understand that he'd feel so much more if he opened up completely?

He shuddered, rigid, his groan wrenched out from deep within. She wrapped her arms and legs tight around him. Kissed the side of his face over and over. He'd buried it deep into her neck. She turned into him, wanting to kiss his beautiful mouth. But he kept it locked in the ridge above her collar-bone. So she kissed the skin she did have access to—his neck, his jaw, his cheek. She paused—sure she'd tasted salt. Sweat or tears? Maybe both.

'Rhys?'

Silence. For long moments she felt his heart thunder against hers, felt his ragged breathing. Finally he pulled out, pushed away. Stood. Said nothing. Took a towel and left.

She lay where she was, on the floor, the streaming water keeping her warm, washing away the taste of her own tears.

CHAPTER ELEVEN

BY THE time Sienna braved the bedroom Rhys had already finished there. She pulled on some clothes, feeling colder than she had the entire time in Sydney. Summoning courage, she walked into the living area. He was standing by the window, looking out through the thin lines of the blinds. He must have heard her because he turned immediately.

'I was thinking Thai for dinner. What do you say?'

She stared at him. The smile was there, there was even a slight twinkle in his eye. But his heart was missing.

Her own heart sank. Useless. She'd tried and failed. He'd never let her beyond the barriers and into the reserves he held so deep. She shook her head a little. Such a shame. He was a man who could offer so much—to someone. If only he'd stop for a second and let that someone in. But it wasn't going to be her. And, she acknowledged sadly, nor should it be. She was going beyond her own boundaries as it was. Why blur his as well?

'Tell me about your trip.'

So she was going to be doing the talking—again. And she did. Talked to him about the plans for South America, her desire to see the ancient Inca settlement. Then she was due to fly to London. Hopefully get some work there. Maybe travel about a bit. Ireland? The Continent? She really didn't know but she kept up the chatter. Not wanting the situation to descend into awkward silence. A couple of times he looked about to say something. Then stopped. She looked away, tried to ignore her own hurt. He wouldn't talk to her. He wouldn't trust her. He couldn't love her. The sense of futility grew. There was no point any more. And she shouldn't hang around to go from bruised to broken.

Rhys found the curry utterly tasteless. Might as well be chewing cardboard. This slop was from his favourite Thai restaurant? Maybe he was coming down with something and his taste buds were the first to be infected. He watched Sienna spoon more sauce onto her rice. She was talking, as much as usual, but with restraint. Being careful not to cross any lines. He knew she was holding back over what had happened in the bathroom. In her particularly unique way she'd asked him about the scar, invited him to confess to her. And the thing was he'd been tempted, so tempted. Still was. But it wasn't possible. That was what had made him so angry.

He knew he hadn't hurt her in a physical sense. The way her hips had risen to meet his, matching his energy, his rhythm. The way her hands had pressed him closer, the way she had cried his name as sensation had overruled everything. Despite his anger, his lack of finesse, she had still taken him, enveloping him in her softness, wanting him no matter what. It made him think that maybe, even if she knew it all, she'd still embrace him. That thought was so heady, so intoxicating, he could hardly reason. He wanted it—to confide in her, to take her comfort. And he was beginning to think he wanted it long-term.

But it couldn't happen. He drank deeply from his glass of

water. Trying to cool down, calm down. It ripped him apart that the one person to whom he longed to give everything was so vulnerable. And her vulnerability would make him vulnerable. And that he couldn't allow.

So he couldn't talk about it. He tried to switch back to usual mode—of trying to forget it at all times. Some things ran too deep ever to be touched, not by her. Yet somehow she'd got so close. He'd had to push back—barely hiding the hurt. He just wanted to feel better. Wanted to find that physical relief.

But it was only temporary. And now he felt worse.

He pushed his plate away, overcome by a sense of foreboding. Something really, really bad was going to happen if she went on that trip. He knew it in his bones. 'Are you sure you should do it?'

'Do what?'

He'd interrupted her mid-flow and was ashamed to admit he hadn't caught up with her last sentence. He was still struggling with the whole concept. 'Your trip. South America.'

'I'm sorry?'

'Are you sure it's wise? I mean, maybe you're not up to it yet.'

'Not up to it? What do you mean not up to it?'

He'd got her back up just like that. He wasn't getting this out right. 'I—'

'Are you saying you don't think I can do it?'

'No, but—'

'Don't you dare lecture me on what I can and can't do.'

The snap came quicker and sharper than he'd anticipated. 'Peru isn't the easiest of destinations. The ruins will be wonderful but it's a hard trek—the path to the top outlook is steep and narrow.'

'So?'

'You have a heart condition, Sienna. You have to be careful when travelling at altitude. You're not trekking all the way up there, are you?' His mind sped into medic mode. 'What about antibiotics? Have you got some with you? You're at greater risk of—'

'I'm well aware of what I'm at risk of. I don't need you to tell me.' She put her fork down. 'You might be a doctor, Rhys, but you're not my doctor.'

'I'm not lecturing you in my professional capacity. I'm talking common sense.' He glared at her. 'You're a woman travelling alone. What if you got in trouble?'

'Oh, please, we're living in the twenty-first century. Women travel alone everywhere all the time.'

'That doesn't make it sensible. I'd be saying the same thing if you were going Outback or to Asia or…anywhere.' He clamped his jaw shut and glared some more. Anger continued to rise. What the hell was she doing on this trip anyway? What about her friends, her family, her life? 'Even your mates at the hostel travel with someone. Why aren't you doing this with a friend?'

'That's the whole point, Rhys. I want to do this on my own.' Hurt glistened in her eyes and he knew it wasn't just from this line of conversation. 'I don't need anyone, Rhys.'

'But you might. What if you have an accident? What if you get in trouble?'

'I'm not going to get in trouble. I am not weak, Rhys. I can do anything.'

'Fine! Smash your head against that wall. Go on. Do it. Just to prove you can.' He pointed to the wall dividing the kitchen from the living room. 'No? Not going to? Because it's a dumb thing to do. And so is jetting off to who knows where all by yourself. A dumb thing to do.'

'It is not. This is what I want.' Her eyes were bright. 'I want this. I'm leaving. I'm living my life. *Mine*. I'm not sharing it.

And I will not be told what I can and can't do by you or anyone else. OK?'

'Well, I…' *don't want you to* '…think it's stupid,' he said lamely.

'Well, we're just going to have to agree to disagree.' She pushed her plate away, food half eaten. 'Maybe I should go back to the hostel.'

'No!' He felt like banging her head on the wall for her. 'No.' He repeated it, less loud but just as vehement. He thought of another point. 'There are snakes there, you know. Lots and lots of snakes. And spiders. Big ones.'

'Why are you doing this?' She positively smoked at him. 'We have a few hours left, Rhys. Can't we just enjoy it? Forget about my trip. Why do you want to ruin this last day?'

Good question. Why did he? Because it was all wrong. Everything felt wrong all of the time. Except when he was deep inside her. Then it was all very, very right. But that couldn't be right. She was not the one to want more from. He was filled with the desperate need to be with her and the stark knowledge that it couldn't be for any more than this one last night. No way could it be more. He could not take the risk.

He stood up from the table so fast he knocked over his chair. 'Forget it. Forget everything. Let's not waste another minute.'

But the hesitation in her face was unmistakable now. That first night, it had been the merest flicker, gone again under the weight of desire. Now, he saw, the desire had been stamped out by the burden of insecurity. He didn't blame her but still he tried. He speared her gaze with his as he stepped forward, wanting the physical attraction to overrule their heads and hearts. He wanted to hold her close, kiss her, make the doubts disappear in the heat of the moment. Just once more.

Her gaze slid away, avoiding him. He'd held back and now she was shutting him out. He understood but he hated it. He wanted to restore her openness, her wide-eyed honesty. But to do that, he'd have to be the honest, open one.

Could he give just a little of what she was asking? Could he talk to her? She seemed to offer so much if he did.

He ran his fingers through her hair. Wanting to imprint the feel of her, the scent of her, the very essence of her, in his mind and body.

He was so close to caving in, so close to confessing. So torn. Wanting to trust her. Knowing he shouldn't. What had she said? Relationships didn't start this way. Could there be the level of trust he needed? Could he commit to someone who might not be around for as long as he needed?

He pushed away the thoughts, concentrated on actions, on sensations. He traced the line of her jaw with his finger. Nudged her chin so she faced him again, but her lashes brushed her cheek and she wouldn't lift them.

Sienna. His blue-eyed Siren. Even now, in silence, she called to him. Tempting him to surrender that which he had locked away for so long—his secrets, his heart. He inched nearer. If he kissed her the passion would override the promise of the tranquillity that might come if he talked with her. But, much as he wanted to taste her, a piece would still be missing and finally the need to fix things was stronger. He wanted to explain, just a little—wanted to right the wrong inside. Wanted her to understand why this could only be physical, and only for now.

Still she wouldn't meet his gaze. It made him feel worse than anything. He didn't want her to step away. Didn't want her to go back to the hostel. He needed to buy some time. They needed respite from this all-consuming intensity.

He twirled her hair some more. Became aware of the way

she was standing so still before him. Almost as if she was holding her breath.

'Why don't we go see a movie?' he muttered. 'We could go for coffee after and…' Silence fell again. He lightly stroked across her high cheekbones, the silky soft skin so smooth under his fingertips.

'And what?' Her prompt was quiet. Her expression still hidden.

'Talk.' He wanted to. God, the longing. Her lashes swooped up. Her eyes were like deep pools and he wanted to bathe in their healing beauty. Still the fear held him back—the pain of loss and the desperate need to avoid more of that kind of pain. The pressure in his chest was immense. Everything was bubbling so close to the surface, closer than it had ever been. And he wanted to be free of it. But his burden was heavy and she was so slight and he couldn't quite be sure. Not yet.

She was silent a long time.

'Please. Just something light. I know a great café for after. The music's not too loud and it has comfy sofas you can curl up in.' If she curled at one end he could sit beside her. Maybe he could touch her hand, or toy with her hair, and maybe, just maybe, he could talk to her about what had happened on the day that everything had changed.

Don't walk out on me just yet.

What he had to say might hurt her, but if he didn't try he'd probably hurt her even more. And even though this had to come to an end, he didn't want to upset her more than he had to.

'OK.' She put a hand to her chaotic hair. 'Let me go and freshen up.'

He felt a spurt of relief, an easing in the ribcage, sent her a small smile. 'I'll find out what's on.'

She left the room and after a deep breath he went to the kitchen counter where he'd chucked the mail that had been delivered with lunch. He pushed around the stack of letters and the advertising circulars and found the day's paper in the pile. Unfolded it and started leafing through the pages to find the entertainment section. He got to the social pages. Stopped. Stared at his own face in full colour. They were on the beach and he was looking at her and his feelings were there for the world to read. On the other side of the headline was another picture of Sienna alone—smiling straight at the camera.

MAITLAND'S MYSTERY MATCH

Single women of Sydney sigh with despair over this. It seems the city's hottest bachelor has been snagged at last. Rhys Maitland, heir to the Maitland millions, was snapped in his favourite haunt with a strawberry-blonde who, as the pictures show, had him spellbound. What began as an ill-concealed argument became a tentative reconciliation with the blonde giving him a hard time. They finally left the tapas bar and walked to Rhys' nearby luxury apartment—where the Maitland magic must have worked as the blinds have yet to be opened!

Our source tells us Rhys checked into the hostel she was staying at, determined to catch up with the beauty. And as our pictures show, he certainly did that…

Rhys stopped reading, stared sightlessly across the kitchen as it sank in. Source. Sienna. The drivel was merely an add-on to the steamy photo of them kissing on the beach the morning they'd failed to play volleyball. He'd been taken for a ride. Once was unfortunate. Twice was sheer stupidity.

The fear that had been raging within rose and transformed into a fury that was blinding. With excessive force he scrunched the paper in his hands.

Sienna ran the brush through her hair and tried not to let the feeling of elation grow beyond all proportion. Take it easy. Keep it slow.

Something had changed. Her lover, with the world's most impenetrable security system around his heart, might just be about to unlock a gate—a cat-flap, perhaps. A tiny opening into the vast reservoir on the other side. He was so very strong but just then he'd softened—a slight touch. There was hope. She couldn't help but hope. All too easily she flicked her own doubts out of her mind. Focusing on him, she could forget about her own rules.

She jumped out of her skin when she heard him shout her name.

He appeared in the doorway. 'You're just like all the rest, aren't you?'

'Rhys?' Shocked, she watched as he strode towards her, his hands shaking. He shoved the newspaper in her face. She grasped it but couldn't read—too thrown by his expression, the menace with which he towered over her.

'Is that what you were writing earlier? More details you can sell for part two of your exposé?'

'Rhys, what are you talking about?' Frantic, she glanced down over the headline, saw the picture of herself looking so cheekily at whomever it was taking the photo. Oh, no. 'Rhys, this wasn't me.'

'Yeah, right. When did you tip them off? You've known all along, haven't you?' He swore. 'God, how guilty I felt. I really thought I'd hurt you. And you've been laughing at me this whole time.' He stepped back, strode around the room.

'You've played me for such a fool. What is it you're really after—fifteen minutes of fame? Money?'

'Rhys, look at me.' He couldn't think this had been her. He just couldn't.

'Look at you? Like I am there—*in love?*' Bitterly scornful, he stopped pacing, gestured to the paper. 'Never.' He spun away, swore some more—ferociously.

She shrank from the vehemence in his voice and the frown on his face. Violently hurt by his words and how quick he was to believe so badly of her. For a second their gazes met—steel lancing tremulous blue.

'No, don't give me that look. Your eyes tell lies.' He turned away from her again, fingers curling back into fists. 'How could I have been so stupid?'

'Rhys—' Panicked that he wouldn't stop and think.

'Take the rubbish you helped them write and go.'

'Rhys!' She had to talk to him. Had to get her head round what the hell had happened, but he was wild and wasn't going to listen and wasn't giving her a second.

'I can't believe I was such an idiot. And to think I wanted to tell you…to think I was going to—' He turned sharply and headed to the door.

'What, Rhys?' she cried after him. Her voice breaking as she tried to make him stop, make him hear her. 'Whatever it is you can tell me!'

'I can't!' He whirled to face her. Stepped towards her with such barely held fury she instinctively moved back. He shouted. Every word wounded. 'I can't trust you!'

She stared into his face. Cringing at the blazing anger, the hate she saw there. Crushing hurt swamped her. Her heart ached so hard she thought it would burst. She couldn't take any more. She wanted to give to him. Wanted him to lean on her the way she had him.

She wanted to love him.

And he thought she'd betrayed him?

They could offer billions and she'd never let him down. But she could say nothing. Do nothing. Could only try to escape the absolute agony she felt at his words. She wanted to hide from the bitter way he looked at her. Wanted to hide from the fact he'd never care for her the way she did for him. Oh, how that hurt.

She tried to bite back the sobs, but they burst out anyway. Deep, racking gulps that stole her fight and her energy. Hardly able to see, she grabbed at her bag, crushing the pages of the paper against her. Scalding tears spilled. Blindly she ran.

CHAPTER TWELVE

THE emergency department was overflowing as always. Rhys had rung in. Not wanting a minute more of his wretched holiday, so out of sorts and unhappy that he'd be best off working crazy hours and having something—anything—to occupy his brain and fill in the void where his heart should be. He needed a sense of purpose—saving a few lives ought to be enough. Wasn't that the whole reason he went into medicine? To make amends?

Despite the fact he was busy he still felt hollow—lonely in the crowded corridors. He dealt with crises and walked through the waiting areas. Used to recognition in the eyes of passers-by, he was able to let the obvious speculation slide over him. He kept up his reserved but amiable demeanour. Hid behind the 'Doctor' title. He watched the patients, the worried faces of family and lovers, witnessed the reunions, the fears, the loss, the relief, the recovery.

Usually he drew satisfaction from the effort of his work. Even if he failed to help someone, he knew he had tried. And it tired him enough to keep the demons at bay. But now it wasn't working. Instead the emptiness inside was growing.

He was haunted.

In every patient he saw the hurt in her eyes. The plea to

stop, the shock, the truth. And with every passing moment the certainty grew that he'd been so wrong. So completely wrong he didn't know how he was going to make it right.

He ignored the sidelong grins and glances of his colleagues. They were his friends. He knew he had their respect. But he also knew their curiosity would get the better of them. It was Tim—inevitably—who broached the topic as they walked through the ward. 'So you really hit it off with the drummer girl.'

Rhys gave a noncommittal grunt and hoped it was enough to signal 'end of conversation'.

'What was the surgery?'

Rhys frowned. 'Surgery?'

'You know, the pictures in the paper.'

Pictures. He hadn't got much past the opening paragraph. Hadn't seen beyond the teasing grin she'd given the camera. There'd been other pictures?

Tim drummed his fingers on his chest. 'I'm thinking heart?'

'Valve replacement,' Rhys answered shortly. 'I have to go check something.'

He strode to the staff room, rifled through the stack of papers and magazines on the table. *Please, please, please.* And there it was. Folded open, well read by the look of it. Gritting his teeth, he skimmed over the first few lines, going straight to the later paragraphs.

No stranger to tragedy, has Rhys set himself up for more heartache by falling for one of his patients?

He froze, icy fingers slipping across his skin. He looked for the first time at the photos along the bottom of the page. They'd snapped her in his shirt when they were on the beach in the pale light of dawn. It was only buttoned at the waist—she looked hot and there was no hiding her fresh-from-bed hair. And there was no hiding her scar in the open vee of his shirt either. To make it worse they'd blown up the part of her chest and added it as a pop-up pic, circling the mark of the long incision.

The scar suggests the mystery beauty has had major surgery.

Hot guilt mixed with the icy dread. The words confirmed what he already knew. What had kept him tossing and turning at night. Sienna would never have sold him out.

His knuckles clenched, the skin turning white as he read on. Media intrusion was something he was used to. He disliked it and worked hard to avoid it, but it came with his name. She had no experience, had no defences built for this kind of invasion. They had no right to destroy her privacy. She would hate to have her scar revealed to the world.

He had been such an idiot. She must surely hate him. She should have been angry, should have yelled, should have put him in his place good and proper. But she'd been hurt—too hurt. And he'd been a fool to throw away someone who could care like that.

He should have been helping her—consoling her over having her life ripped open for the entertainment of the masses. Instead he'd accused her of orchestrating the whole thing.

And why? He'd been like a trapped tiger searching out something to attack. It gave him a way of shoving her back. Because he'd been on the verge of letting her right inside and it terrified him.

He raked fingers through his hair as frustration and futility ravaged his heart. Sienna hadn't deserved that, just as she didn't deserve this. She'd be mortified by these pictures. He looked closely at the head and shoulders shot of her at the top of the page—the one where she smiled so freely. He could make out part of the sign on the wall behind her. Recognised it hung in Reception at the hostel. Of course, it was obvious now. Curtis—who had to work all those hours because he 'needed the money'. He'd known all along who Rhys was. The creep. With sadness Rhys read on. Not only had they debated on her history, they'd printed the details of his accident with Theo. And then they'd reprinted some of Mandy's more painful comments. He blanched as he skimmed over them. So inevitable. So predictable. So true?

Sienna read the article again and again and again. She had no chance of sleeping on the plane. Couldn't concentrate on any in-flight entertainment. The cabin steward was wonderfully kind and provided an entire box of tissues and a cool pack for her eyes.

Rhys, fourteen at the time, and his twelve-year-old cousin Theo were skateboarding down the street. A car, speeding out of its driveway, collided with both boys. Rhys was tossed to the side while Theo was crushed, dying at the scene…

She stared at the photos, not of herself, but of Rhys, of the way he was smiling at her—in love? So the gushing journalist said. But she knew otherwise. He'd *told* her otherwise. He'd never opened up. She'd asked. He'd refused. Not trusting in himself, in her, or in the bond she'd thought they had. All the while she'd been so open, he'd kept part of himself locked away. But what else could she expect when they'd started so casually? She couldn't demand anything more serious from him just because she then wanted it.

She wished it had stayed purely physical—that searing attraction. It had been a wild coming together that had blown her mind. In the hostel they'd channelled the energy, deliberately fuelling it, pushing it. Since the first time in his apartment, she'd been unable to control anything, not least the entirety of her response.

For it was no longer just physical. Her mind was involved. And so was her heart. And all she could hear right now was her head telling her how bad her heart was feeling.

His ex-girlfriend Mandy says he's emotionally crippled, claiming the city's wealthiest bachelor will never wed as he's already married to his job...

Deep anger gripped her as she read the comments. No wonder he was so untrusting, when his ex could so blithely say such cutting things. He wasn't crippled, he was warm and caring and funny and *hurt*.

Now she knew his history she saw it had been for the best. They could never have had a relationship beyond a brief affair. She couldn't give him what he needed—serenity, security, stability. There were things on her list that she'd never written down. Rules she had to live by—no marriage, no kids. She couldn't promise her life to anyone, not when she wasn't sure she had the power to see it through. But she needed to be a little better at observing those rules. Instinctively she'd known long-term wasn't for her, thinking it was because she didn't want anyone else to worry over her the way her mother and brother did. But now she knew the real reason was because she couldn't cope with the heartache herself. She just wasn't strong enough. And she couldn't bear to see Rhys hurt more than he already was. He needed someone whole and well and who would be reliable. She couldn't guarantee that. She didn't know what her future held.

Their parting was definitely for the best.

That didn't stop the tears rolling.

Taking several deep breaths, Rhys ducked into the supply cupboard for some space, raised shaking fingers to his face and massaged his forehead. *Sienna, Sienna, Sienna.*

He could no longer keep the lid on his emotions. For the first time his personal life was affecting his ability to work. He'd almost choked up over that patient. Had seen the startled look the nurse had given him. He couldn't go on like this. Every second it got worse, not better.

He closed his eyes and caught the memory of when he'd first seen her.

The blood had pumped in his veins. His senses had gone supersonic. Everything was brighter when she was around. Hell, he was pathetic. He'd made up the whole Monroe thing to escape himself more than anything. It wasn't about her. It had been about him. And it had backfired completely.

His world was all about life and death. He witnessed both—every day, every night. But that was just it, he was witnessing. Facilitating. Fighting for others. But not actually doing it himself. He'd been driven to make a difference—to give, to help. But he was so busy trying to save, he no longer lived his own life. He stood on the sidelines, spectating. Bound by fear. Afraid of losing. But he'd already lost.

Sienna had been forced to spectate for most of her life. He had chosen to. Now she was fighting to live it—reaching out and taking it on with both hands. Rhys couldn't, he felt duty-bound not to waste the life he'd been given. Not when he'd been instrumental in Theo losing his. He'd work and help and never be useless again.

But didn't he have a duty to Sienna as well? At the very least, she deserved an explanation and an apology. He couldn't leave it unfinished. He owed her answers. He owed her honesty.

He banged his creased forehead with his knuckles. She didn't want duty from him. She'd said he had a responsibility to live his own life. What about his life's to-do list? He'd never even thought about it seriously. He'd never been to Peru either. Why shouldn't he go too? Wasn't it as much a waste of a life to focus so completely on only one aspect—in his case, work? Shouldn't he be embracing all avenues of his life? How she tempted him. Made him long for everything.

In the gloom of the supply room it dawned on him that he'd used her—wanting the moments of bliss to break up the lifetime of guilt. And hadn't she used him too? To have those moments of freedom? Be treated normally? But then she'd wanted more—she'd wanted him to open up to her. Why? If it was just a fling, an affair—an extended one-night stand...

Because it wasn't just a fling. Because she cared.

And he'd hurt her. And in hurting her, he'd hurt himself more. The least he could do was apologise. See her, explain it all the best he could. He'd never been able to apologise to Theo. He should take the opportunity to apologise to her while he had it. He had to take a leaf out of her book and seize the day. Make the most of every moment, and leave no room for regret. He locked his knuckles together. Right now he re-gretted everything he hadn't done.

He didn't know what the future held. No one did. All he knew was that he couldn't go on in the present as it was. He couldn't hide any more. It was too late. She was already there, lodged deep in his heart, and he had to fight to stop his heart from breaking.

A nurse came into the cupboard. Stopped as she saw Rhys

leaning against the cabinet. Glanced round to see if there was anyone else in the tiny room. 'Sorry, I—'

'It's OK. I was just leaving.'

CHAPTER THIRTEEN

SOMEHOW it was so typical that after five days of fairly tiring travel, a lifetime of dreaming and a huge chunk of her life savings spent, the ruins of Machu Picchu would be shrouded in mist the one day Sienna had to visit them. She'd known it would be a possibility, it wasn't the optimum time to travel there weather-wise, but she'd wanted to go so much and hadn't wanted to wait any longer. She'd wanted it to be the first major step on her big adventure. New year, new life. But she'd stepped into her adventure with far more of a jump than she'd planned.

And there would be no view for her. Not today. She wouldn't be climbing the steep track. The one that Rhys had become so 'lecturing doctor' over. She hadn't wanted to anyway, she'd just wanted to walk in the ancient ruins and marvel. And she hadn't trekked all the way. She'd taken the train, taken her time, got used to the thinner air, ensured she rested as well as she could. Despite what he thought, she knew her own limitations. And it was enough to be here. Wasn't it?

But the void couldn't be filled—no view to fill it, no one to share it, no one to laugh about it. She was mad with him for ruining what should have been one of her life's most marvellous moments. Mad with herself for letting him.

She sat in the damp air and wallowed. She was pathetic. Other tourists walked on by. She hadn't banded together with any of them. Just wanted her own company—as she'd told Rhys. But she'd lied. She'd wanted his.

Finally she stood, deciding to go down to the village below where she was staying. Maybe she could add another day there, hope for better weather tomorrow. She could laze in the thermal pools this afternoon and try to jolly herself out of it.

As she went she saw someone walking up the other way.

He was staring straight at her. Not smiling. Not frowning. Just looking kind of frozen. Oh, man, she was hallucinating. Thought it was him. Wishful thinking. She blinked a few times. Maybe she had some weird form of altitude sickness?

'Sienna.' Not a question, but a call—a command for attention.

'Rhys?' For the first time in years she nearly fainted. She consciously tensed every muscle in her body, refusing to let the light recede. 'What are you doing here?'

He didn't reply until he was right in front of her. He really was there. Wearing khaki trousers, a long-sleeved tee and at least three days' stubble. 'There was something I wanted to tell you.'

She waited—for once in her life struck dumb.

As Rhys drew in his breath, all the sentences he'd mentally rehearsed in the aeroplane disappeared into the mist. 'I, uh, didn't want you to go.' With relief he saw the colour flood back into her cheeks.

'Pardon?' She stood, feet planted firmly on the ground, in front of him.

The words forced their way out from deep inside. 'I didn't want you to leave. I wanted you to stay.' He puffed the air out. There. He'd done it. He'd said it.

She whirled on him. 'That's it? That's all you have to say?'

She unzipped the pocket to the side of her thigh, pulled out the wrinkled pages from the paper.

'I'm sorry I thought…I'm sorry I couldn't…I'm sorry.' He wanted to talk but the words weren't coming. The blockage in his chest had risen to his throat and it hurt. He just wanted to reach out and pull her home to his embrace. If he could hold her tight to him, maybe he could whisper it all in her ear. God, how he needed her comfort and how he longed to comfort her. She was close enough to touch but she was looking mad and now words were flying from her.

'You know, you're the one who needs the surgery. You're the one whose heart needs cutting open—to free the blockages. Let the blood flow. Let the love flow.' Tears spilled down her face; the pages rustled in her shaking hands. 'I opened up to you—really opened up. And you held back from me the whole time.' She sniffed, scrubbed a tear away with a fist. 'Even when you told me who you were, you still held back.'

Defensive anger rose. 'No, I didn't. Not in bed. I gave you everything there and you know it.' He'd shown her, again and again.

'So what about sex, Rhys? There was more to us than sex. Don't you get it? It would never have been that fantastic if there wasn't more.'

He stopped. Of course there was more than sex—that was just one tangible facet of a deeply profound bond. They connected on many levels, not just the physical. He ran his hands through his hair. This wasn't going anything like he'd imagined. He was supposed to have apologised to her and then it would all have been OK. He'd tried to prepare. Knew he'd have to talk. But now it had come to the moment, he still didn't know how to say it, didn't know where to start.

'I just wanted to forget it all.' He ached to enfold her in his arms, needing to feel her length against his. To be certain they weren't ever separating again.

'Trying to forget doesn't work—*does it?*' She stared at him sadly.

He looked away from the accusation in her gaze, the astuteness, the question she'd asked before and would ask again. She'd pierced through. He could feel his tension building, demanding to be let out at last. He'd come so far for her. He was already committed. And if he didn't talk now, he'd lose her.

'Actually I have a photographic memory.' A slight lift of his shoulders as he started. 'And like an elephant, I can't forget.'

After a stretch she spoke again, softer this time. 'What can't you forget?'

He looked up the path to where she stood square on, facing him. Slim but so strong. Stronger than he'd ever imagined. Those brilliant blue eyes of hers stared intensely, seeing right through him, willing him to share his burden. The ultimatum—giving him no choice.

And finally he did it. Told her. The one thing he'd never told anyone—the awful truth. 'It was my fault.'

'What?'

He glanced at the paper in her hand. 'My cousin. Theo.'

'How?'

He looked down at the ground, not wanting to see her frown. 'We were skateboarding. I was in front. We were racing. A car came out the driveway.'

He'd got such a fright from the noise he'd come off his own board, landed roughly on the edge of the footpath, right on pieces of broken bottle. He'd skidded, the bits of glass embedded deep in his thigh, ribboning the skin and muscle, marking him for life.

'I don't see how it was your fault, Rhys. That car came

flying out of the driveway—straight across the footpath. The driver was the person who was going too fast, who should have stopped to check. You were just playing in your neighbourhood like all kids do.'

'But if I hadn't challenged Theo to a race. If I hadn't been showing off and going so fast, calling out to him to hurry. We didn't hear the car. He was asking me to wait up and I didn't—'

He broke off suddenly. Head bowed, he tried to fix his blurry vision by focusing on one tuft of grass poking through the muddied track. Cold sweat slid over him. And as he talked he didn't know if she could hear him any more. All he felt was the agony. The fear. 'I couldn't do anything. I couldn't help him. I just sat there and held his hand and watched while he slipped away. He looked at me and then he just—'

They'd tried to tell him Theo wouldn't have known anything. But Rhys knew better. He'd seen it in his eyes, seen the plea for help.

He hated going over this. Hated the memories. Wanted to keep it all buried deep where he could try to forget about it. Even though he failed day in, day out. But trying to forget was better than grinding through this rotting mess that tasted foul as he spoke of it. *If only, if only, if only.* Thousands of times he'd replayed it. Thousands of hours feeling horror and dread and guilt.

'And now you're a doctor.'

She understood already but still he voiced it, realising now how much he *wanted* to tell her, hoping comfort would come with confessing everything. 'I was so useless. He was dying and I couldn't do anything. I won't be in that position again. At least now I can try to help. Not do *nothing.*'

* * *

Sienna longed to touch him, wanted to wrap her arms around him, but he stood so defensively. Not looking at her, fists clenched, sweat shining on his forehead. She saw how hard this was for him. How deep the feelings were buried. While she didn't want to stop the flow, she couldn't let him go on blaming himself. She stepped a little closer.

'You didn't do nothing, Rhys. You held him. You were there for him. You were with him. He wasn't alone.' That, she knew, was huge.

It was Rhys who had been alone. A scared child, burdened with a guilt no one would have expected him to carry. Not many people could handle holding someone who lay dying— not in circumstances like that, not without help. She understood his mission now, the need that drove him to work in the field he did, with the dedication he had. So busy fighting he'd forgotten how to have fun.

Her heart ached—for him, and for her. He'd paid a price high enough—he didn't need to be with someone who might only cost him more. She breathed little, quick breaths, trying to be strong. Maybe they could talk. It might help. But after that she knew she had to walk away.

She definitely didn't want a heart that worked properly if it was going to hurt this bad.

'How many?' She focused on him.

'How many what?'

'How many do you have to save before you feel better about Theo? You can't bring him back.'

'I know that.'

'It wasn't your fault. You were a kid—you weren't responsible for him. The person responsible was the person behind the wheel of the car.'

He stood like a statue and she had no idea whether she was getting through to him.

'You can't go beating yourself up over this the rest of your life. I'm sure he'd hate that.'

He flinched. She couldn't tell what he was thinking. The silence grew and this time she waited.

'I just wanted to help him.' The words came out low and so full of need she could hear the bleed in his heart and the tears in his soul.

Very gently she replied, 'You did.'

'How was the view from the top?'

Change of topic. That was as much as she was going to get. He was so on edge she didn't know whether to push much more. He stood rigid as he battled to keep everything in.

'I didn't go up.' She gestured at the mist. 'Didn't seem much point with the weather like this.'

'Will you try tomorrow?'

'I'm supposed to be leaving. But I was thinking I might go up in the helicopter in the morning, if it's a clear day.'

He swore sharply, long and loud. 'You can't do this.'

Stunned, she stared. 'Do what?'

'Mess me around. You know, you say you're going to go off and do this, that and the other and people who care about you worry the whole time and then you don't do it anyway so they didn't have to worry after all and then you turn around and say maybe you'll do something even more stupid and then they have to worry all over again.'

She frowned, flummoxed by the verbal onslaught she'd never have expected from him. People who cared about her? Her family didn't even know she was here. The only person who knew she was here was—

'Who cares about me, Rhys? Why are you so worried about my heart?'

'It's not your heart I'm worried about!' he roared. 'It's

mine!' His tension snapped. Anger, frustration and uncontrollable emotion poured out of him as he stood in the path and yelled. 'I worry about you. I want to take care of you. That's what people who love each other do. It's not because I think you're sick. It's because I love you!'

He stopped. The sound of his passion reverberated around them.

How could it be that those three little words could have one half of her soaring higher than the sky-touching peaks around them and the other half of her sinking fast into despair and remorse? Raw honesty shone in his face. He was utterly exposed, had opened up completely, for her—inviting her into a place she had no right to be.

What had she done?

'You can't expect me to just sit back and agree to whatever stupid scheme you've come up with,' he growled, muscles bunching. 'You can't do this emotional blackmail thing— accusing me of mollycoddling when I'm just pointing out common sense.'

Her silly bruised and battered heart beat stronger than it ever had. But her brain screamed—she was wicked to have let this happen. She wished she'd known about his past sooner. She'd have stayed away then, steered well clear so she wouldn't hurt him.

'Sienna, I am *sick* of this talking.' He strode towards her, words abandoned as his body went into action.

'Rhys.' She stumbled and he swiftly pulled her into his arms.

His grip hurt and he lifted her clear off her feet. His mouth pressed hard on hers. And it was so wonderful it blocked the fears scurrying in her head. For a spell it was simply bliss. She reached up with both hands, threading them through his thick hair, and strained to give as well as to take. He raked in her body, pressing her close with a hug that was so tight she struggled to suck air into her squeezed lungs. She couldn't tell who was shaking more. He was muttering, the words muffled as he kissed her face. It took several moments, many kisses, to decipher what it was he was saying again and again.

'Don't.'

'Don't what?'

'Don't go without me.'

'Rhys.' She pushed with all her might, pulling her head away and raising tortured eyes to him. 'I can't promise you that.'

CHAPTER FOURTEEN

'LET'S go.' She pulled away from Rhys, starting to head down the track.

He looked stunned. 'Sienna—'

'That site guard has been looking at us like we're loco and about to leap onto the ruins and do something sacrilegious.'

'If kissing you is sacrilegious, then I intend to be the biggest sinner there is.' His mouth moved into a sort of smile but his eyes showed his seriousness—and uncertainty. 'OK, now we have to talk about this. You have to talk.'

'I know and I will. Let's just do it somewhere private, OK?' She didn't want to stand in the middle of a major tourist attraction, pour her heart out to the love of her life, and then walk away from him. She needed privacy. So did he.

She walked briskly to the entrance to the ruins and got straight on the waiting bus. It wasn't a long trip down to the town below the ruins, but today it would take for ever.

'Sienna.'

She didn't want to look at him, didn't want to be tempted. She had to be strong—it was for his own good, damn it. But she hated herself. He'd just told her he loved her and here she was running again, leaving him hanging. She blinked, wanting rid of the sting in her eyes. She spoke quickly, not wanting stilted silence. He didn't deserve that. 'How did you get here?'

'Helicopter.'

'Helicopter?' Amazed, she spun to look at him then. 'Why?'

'I needed to get here quickly.'

'You haven't had time to acclimatise. You might get altitude sickness.'

'It's not the altitude that's making me feel...' His voice trailed away.

Hurriedly she turned back and looked out the window, her cheeks flaming. Her innards had gone mushy and she fought to maintain her resolve. Only then did she realise how hard he was going to make this.

As the bus moved she chanced another look at him. Less stunned. A lot determined. She had a fight on her hands, but for his sake she'd better win it. She couldn't bear to hurt him more than he already had been. Guilt ripped through her. She had forced him to open up. She loved him for it. But wasn't being with her going to hurt him beyond repair?

'I'm sorry they showed your scar.' He nodded at the pages still in her hand.

She shrugged. 'It's OK. I guess I'm never going to escape it.'

'No, but you'll learn to live with it. It's only a small part of who you are, Sienna.'

She looked at him keenly. 'Ditto.'

She led him to her hotel, straight in and up the stairs to her room.

He looked about, took in the double bed. 'No dorm room this time?'

'I needed some space.'

She recognised the glint in his eye and moved back into the other half of the room. She needed space from *him* now. If he came any nearer she'd melt into his arms. Not allowed. She had to think of him rather than herself. She picked up her journal, waved it at him like a sword. 'New year, new journal, new me.' She laughed—bitter and brittle. 'I wrote my list, as you know. But there were some things I didn't write down. The really important things.' She took a deep breath. 'I can't be with someone for ever, Rhys. I can't ever have kids or a family or anything like that. I decided I was going to live life *now*. I can't make promises for the future—not to anyone.'

'Why not?'

'Because there might not be a future.'

His colour drained. 'What are you saying?'

She sighed. 'I remember when Dad died. Mum was devastated. It nearly killed her too. She was great with us kids but her heart went into the grave with him. You can still see it in her eyes.' She looked to him, pleading for him to understand. 'You've already been through enough, Rhys. You don't need to hook up with someone who might not be around for you. I don't want you to go through that. I don't want to leave a husband without a wife, children without a mother.'

'Who says you will? Who says you won't live to be a hundred? Hell, bits of your heart are practically bionic. They keep coming up with better treatments all the time. Why do you have dibs on dying first? I could get hit by a bus tomorrow.' His colour had returned, and he flashed his easy smile.

'Don't, Rhys.' He wasn't taking this seriously. And she meant it, she really meant it.

He sobered. 'Sienna, a few days ago I might have agreed with you. But now I know I have to be with you for however long fate decides it is we have together. I thought I couldn't bear a future with you in it. Because of the possibility I might lose you. But the fact is, I can't bear a present without you. I'm alive now. I want to live now.'

He pointed to her chest. 'I know the risks. You know the

risks. They're there but they're not that big. And we're at risk of a million other things we don't even know about. We have to live life, Sienna, for as long as we have it. We have to create life—lives even.' His smile was soft. 'And we have to let them take their courses. No more sidelines.'

He stepped nearer, spoke up some more. 'It isn't your job to protect me. You can't—not like this.' He took the journal from her hand, tossed it onto the floor where it landed with a thud. 'You once told me that people write things down to help make them real. But you didn't write this down. Why?'

She stared. 'Because it was…so fundamental.'

'No.' He shook his head. Took another step nearer, his voice another notch louder. 'It's not. This isn't some goal, Sienna. It isn't meant to happen and you know that.'

The thing she wanted most was the thing she didn't want the most. Torn and trapped by her conflicting emotions and by his relentless advance across the room, she stood immobile and mute.

'No one truly wants a lonely life. Not many people choose to reject the possibility, the hope of love. You say you want to live every moment to the full and yet you won't let someone share it with you? I never thought you of all people would be so defeatist!' With each word his volume increased. They'd be hearing him up at the ruins. Sienna could hardly bear to hear him at all.

'People like me didn't spend years studying, years working to fix you, for you to then chicken out. You are whole, Sienna. And you have to let yourself live a whole life.' He stopped right in front of her, breathing hard, eyes glued to hers.

She was afraid to move. 'I'm broken, Rhys.'

'No, you're not.' He gave a half-smile and a half-shrug. 'No more than me. No more than most other people.'

'You'd always want to take care of me.'

'Of course I would. I love you. And I expect you to take care of me too. But I've never stifled you, Sienna, and I never will. When you're booking your flight in the helicopter, make sure my seat's right next to yours.'

'You want to go with me?'

'Everywhere.'

Her eyes watered. Could she really have it all? For so long she'd thought not and this was too much. She pressed her palms together, tried to take some deeper breaths. She couldn't seem to think any more. She felt frozen on the edge of a precipice and she didn't know if she was going to be able to take the leap.

'You know what I think?'

She looked at him, unable to voice the question.

'I think you're scared. Scared to really let yourself fall.'

Of course she was scared. Terrified. Petrified. Far more fear in her here than any stupid snake or spider could arouse.

'I'm scared too—the whole thing is crazy. We've known each other what—a week? But this is right, you know it is. Let's live *now,* Sienna. Jump with me.'

He wasn't going to let it go. Wasn't going to let her go. She tried to speak. Twisted her lips even. But failed to produce sound.

He stepped nearer. Spoke softly this time. 'It's too late, you know, we're already in free fall.'

At last, squeaky and raw, her voice worked again. 'Do you think either of us remembered a parachute?'

He took her hands in his, held them firm, and smiled. 'Honey, you are my parachute, and I'm yours. So long as we hold onto each other, we'll be fine. I've never been more certain of anything. You've turned me on—and I don't just mean *that.*' He grinned. 'You *make* the trees sing, the air sweet. You make my life. Hell, I don't know how to say it.'

'You're doing OK so far.' The tears overflowed, two fat trails tripping down her cheeks, followed rapidly by twin rivers.

'No fear, remember?'

She returned the grip of his hands, needing to be honest about what frightened her most. 'One day the mechanical bit in this heart might need replacing. I might have to be opened up again.'

'Maybe. And if that happens I'll be holding your hand when you go under.'

Her eyes snapped to his. Intently she focused on him. 'Holding someone's hand can be the best thing you can do for them. The only thing you can do.' She squeezed his tightly, whispered, 'So they're not alone.'

The shadow darkened his eyes and she knew he thought of Theo. 'Yeah.' She knew he understood. The hint of green appeared again as he looked at her. 'Well, I'll be holding your hand when you wake up too.'

She smiled, a little wan, but right back at him. 'Apparently I can get a little stroppy when I wake up.'

He released her, lifting his fingers to frame her face. 'It'll be a good challenge.'

One of her hands crept up and held his to her cheek, the other curled against her chest. 'Then, for as long as it's beating, this heart is staying right beside you.'

The kiss was the sweetest she'd ever experienced. He held her face to his and as their lips joined it was as if their very souls had opened up and embraced. Warm relief mingled with hot desire. Her knowledge that this being together was the beginning of for ever brought an enduring, unlimited joy. She reached for him, caressed him with both gentleness and strength, wanting to express the depth of her feelings.

Inevitably, the sweetness was overtaken by sensual, strident need. But there was a tacit understanding to keep the brakes on for once. They undressed—item by item, as if unveiling everything to each other for the very first time. The love and wonder in his eyes as magnetic as the raw lust that also registered there. When they lay naked on the bed there was nothing but deep kisses for a long, long time. Murmurs of love and mutters of laughter followed. Then no more talking, just action.

His arms, his body, imprisoned hers, but his love didn't bind her. He didn't suffocate her with concern but rather gave her freedom. When she was with him she had the courage to attempt things she'd never before contemplated. While she knew she was whole, having him beside her gave her the push to prove it. Life would never be the same again. Life would never be boring.

'You know, I had some thoughts about what you could do for a job.'

She managed to open an eye and look half enquiring.

'If you were serious about doing something positive, I mean.'

'Yes?' Both eyes opened and she lifted her head a millimetre off the pillow.

'Don't say no straight away. Hear me out.' He sat up on one elbow, enthusiasm seeming to send energy back to his body. 'You know how bored kids in hospital get. How scared?'

'Yes.'

'And you know how much fun it is to make a big, big noise?'

'Yes?'

'Music therapy. I can't believe you haven't thought of it yourself.'

She stared at him blankly. Then her mind worked through the suggestion. 'You mean I go into the hospital and get the kids to bang some drums?'

He beamed. 'Yeah!'

'I can't believe you think I'd want to work in a hospital!'

'Not just any hospital. My hospital. I'll be there.'

'And that makes all the difference?'

'We can have lunch together.'

'As if you take lunch breaks.'

'We can snatch a few moments in the supply room.' He laughed. 'Think about it. You know I'm right.' He stroked her arm. 'You'd be making a difference.'

Her heart flooded and so did her eyes. Again. Actually the idea wasn't bad. She quite liked the possibility of having a van full of xylophones and swanni kazoos and drums and tambourines and noise, noise, noise. She buried her face in his chest, listened to the solid, rhythmic thud of his heart. He was so strong. His drive as a doctor wouldn't be changing. He needed to do it, and he'd sensed that she sought something as challenging and as rewarding for herself. That she wanted to put back in to others' lives as well as her own—just as he did. And he'd worked out a way they could do it together— he wanted her in his world and him in hers, wholly.

He breathed deeply, fingers teasing through her hair. 'Love at first sight. Never thought it happened. Never thought it would happen to me.'

'Tell me about it.' She sighed, contentment cloaking her. 'I walked into that bar and there you were looking ferocious and I blinked and my heart was no longer mine. Just like that.' She nuzzled his neck. 'I love you, Rhys.'

He clamped her to him, arms like a vice, as he spoke low and rough in her ear. 'Marry me, marry me, marry me.'

They lay bonded for a long moment, listening to their quickened breathing, their galloping hearts. She whispered, hardly loud enough for him to hear, hardly able to believe she could feel this happy. 'OK.'

His arms tightened even more. 'No getting out of it now. We'll do it as soon as it can be arranged. The family will want big and pomp and the damn media will want photos.'

She lifted her head to look at him, humour sending a smile to her face. 'That's the real reason you want to marry me, isn't it? So you can bow out of the hellish glare of life as Rhys Maitland, bachelor heir.'

'Darling, you know me so well.'

She rolled her eyes, rolled her hand down his chest, and knew the bliss of limitless love.

The sky was clear and cloudless. One opportunity. Holding her hand tightly, he looked at her and felt an overwhelming sense of togetherness. He hadn't realised just how alone and isolated he'd become. He had a wide circle of friends, an endless supply of dates—had he wanted them—respect and authority at work. He was invited to every party, never stuck for something to do. But, hell, he'd been lonely. There was only one body his arms wanted to encircle. Only one person he wanted to have alongside him.

'We have to draw up a new list.' He saw the question in her eyes and explained. 'We never did get very far on yours. We could check them off—keep up the zest for life.' He grinned. 'I never want to take it for granted. Never want to take us for granted.'

'OK.' She thought for a moment. 'I want to do life-drawing classes. You can be my model.'

'OK.' He'd always be happy to get naked for her. 'I want to make love on a train.'

'Swim with dolphins.'

'Make love on a plane.'

'Be an extra in a movie.'

'Make love on a boat.'

'See the pyramids.'

'Make love on a bus.'

'Go to Rio for the Carnival.'

'Make love on a motorcycle.'

She rolled her eyes. 'Shave my head.'

'Make love in a car.'

'Swim with sharks.'

'Make love in a gondola.'

'Walk on burning embers!'

Undeterred he winked and checked off his fingers. 'Make love in a horse-drawn carriage, a hovercraft, a helicopter.'

'I'm sensing a theme here, Mr One-Track Mind. Haven't you run out of transport options yet?'

'No. Make love in a blimp.'

Giggles erupted from her. 'Gee, that sounds so romantic.'

He turned to her, leaned his face so close their noses brushed. 'Making love with you is *always* the experience of a lifetime.'

Her eyes shone bright. He wanted to tell her again how he loved her, but nothing was needed. She understood. Besides, you couldn't hear a thing above the noise of the rotor blades starting up. The helicopter rose high into the sky. She sat by the window and he was in the middle, nicely anchored with his arms tight around her. They circled around the ruins. Her profile was in the foreground, wisps of her hair fluttered across the blurry backdrop.

The view was incredible.

* * * * *

*Celebrate 60 years of pure reading pleasure
with Harlequin®!*

*Harlequin Presents® is proud to introduce
its gripping new miniseries,*
THE ROYAL HOUSE OF KAREDES.
*An exquisite coronation diamond, split as a symbol of a
warring royal family's feud, is missing! But whoever
reunites the diamond halves will rule all....*

*Welcome to eight brand-new titles that unfold to reveal the
stories of kings and queens, princes and princesses torn
apart by pride and power, but finally reunited by love.*

Step into the world of Karedes with
BILLIONAIRE PRINCE, PREGNANT MISTRESS
Available July 2009 from Harlequin Presents®.

ALEXANDROS KAREDES, SNOW DUSTING the shoulders of his leather jacket and glittering like jewels in his dark hair, stood at the door. Maria felt the blood drain from her head.

"Good evening, Ms. Santos."

His voice was as she remembered it. Deep. Husky. Perfect English, but with the faintest hint of a Greek accent. And cold, as cold as it had been that awful morning she would never forget, when he'd accused her of horrible things, called her terrible names....

"Aren't you going to ask me in?"

She fought for composure. Last time they'd faced each other, they'd been on his turf. Now they were on hers. She was in command here, and that meant everything.

"There's a sign on the door downstairs," she said, her tone every bit as frigid as his. "It says, 'No soliciting or vagrants.'"

His lips drew back in a wolfish grin. "Very amusing."

"What do you want, Prince Alexandros?"

A tight smile eased across his mouth and it killed her that even now, knowing he was a vicious, arrogant man, she couldn't help but notice what a handsome mouth it was. Chiseled. Generous. Beautiful, like the rest of him, which made him living proof that beauty could, indeed, be only skin deep.

"Such formality, Maria. You were hardly so proper the last time we were together."

She knew his choice of words was deliberate. She felt her face heat; she couldn't help that but she damned well didn't have to let him lure her into a verbal sparring match.

"I'll ask you once more, your highness. What do you want?"

"Ask me in and I'll tell you."

"I have no intention of asking you in. Tell me why you're here or don't. It's your choice, just as it will be my choice to shut the door in your face."

He laughed. It infuriated her but she could hardly blame him. He was tall—six two, six three—and though he stood with one shoulder leaning against the door frame, hands tucked casually into the pockets of the jacket, his pose was deceptive. He was strong, with the leanly muscled body of a well-trained athlete.

She remembered his body with painful clarity. The feel of him under her hands. The power of him moving over her. The taste of him on her tongue.

Suddenly, he straightened, his laughter gone. "I have not come this distance to stand in your doorway," he said coldly, "and I am not going to leave until I am ready to do so. I suggest you stand aside and stop behaving like a petulant child."

A petulant child? Was that what he thought? This man who had spent hours making love to her and had then accused her of—of trading her body for profit?

Except it had not been love, it had been sex. And the sooner she got rid of him, the better.

She let go of the doorknob and stepped aside. "You have five minutes."

He strolled past her, bringing cold air and the scent of the night with him. She swung toward him, arms folded. He reached past her, pushed the door closed, then folded his arms, too. She wanted to open the door again but she'd be damned if she was going to get into a who's-in-charge-here argument with him. She was in charge, and he would surely see a tussle over the ground rules as a sign of weakness.

Instead, she looked past him at the big clock above her work table.

"Ten seconds gone," she said briskly. "You're wasting time, your highness."

"What I have to say will take longer than five minutes."

"Then you'll just have to learn to economize. More than five minutes, I'll call the police."

Instantly, his hand was wrapped around her wrist. He tugged her toward him, his dark-chocolate eyes almost black with anger.

"You do that and I'll tell every tabloid shark I can contact about how Maria Santos tried to buy a five-hundred-thousand-dollar commission by seducing a prince." He smiled thinly. "They'll lap it up."

* * * * *

What will it take for this billionaire prince to realize he's falling in love with his mistress…?
Look for
BILLIONAIRE PRINCE, PREGNANT MISTRESS
by Sandra Marton
Available July 2009 from Harlequin Presents®.

We'll be spotlighting a different series every month
throughout 2009 to celebrate our 60th anniversary.

Look for Harlequin® Presents in July!

TWO CROWNS, TWO ISLANDS, ONE LEGACY

A royal family, torn apart by pride and its lust for
power, reunited by purity and passion

Step into the world of Karedes
beginning this July with

BILLIONAIRE PRINCE, PREGNANT MISTRESS

by

Sandra Marton

Eight volumes to collect and treasure!

FORCED TO MARRY

Wives for the taking!

Once these men put a diamond ring on their bride's finger, there's no going back....

Wedlocked and willful, these wives will get a wedding night they'll never forget!

Read all the fantastic stories, out this month in Harlequin Presents EXTRA:

REQUEST YOUR FREE BOOKS!

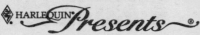 HARLEQUIN *Presents* ®

2 FREE NOVELS PLUS 2 FREE GIFTS!

YES! Please send me 2 FREE Harlequin Presents® novels and my 2 FREE gifts (gifts are worth about $10). After receiving them, if I don't wish to receive any more books, I can return the shipping statement marked "cancel". If I don't cancel, I will receive 6 brand-new novels every month and be billed just $4.05 per book in the U.S. or $4.74 per book in Canada. That's a savings of close to 15% off the cover price! It's quite a bargain! Shipping and handling is just 25¢ per book*. I understand that accepting the 2 free books and gifts places me under no obligation to buy anything. I can always return a shipment and cancel at any time. Even if I never buy another book, the two free books and gifts are mine to keep forever.   106 HDN ERRW 306 HDN ERRL

Name	(PLEASE PRINT)	
Address		Apt. #
City	State/Prov.	Zip/Postal Code

Signature (if under 18, a parent or guardian must sign)

Mail to the **Harlequin Reader Service:**

IN U.S.A.: P.O. Box 1867, Buffalo, NY 14240-1867
IN CANADA: P.O. Box 609, Fort Erie, Ontario L2A 5X3

Not valid to current subscribers of Harlequin Presents books.

Are you a current subscriber of Harlequin Presents books and want to receive the larger-print edition? Call 1-800-873-8635 today!

* Terms and prices subject to change without notice. Prices do not include applicable taxes. Sales tax applicable in N.Y. Canadian residents will be charged applicable provincial taxes and GST. Offer not valid in Quebec. This offer is limited to one order per household. All orders subject to approval. Credit or debit balances in a customer's account(s) may be offset by any other outstanding balance owed by or to the customer. Please allow 4 to 6 weeks for delivery. Offer available while quantities last.

Your Privacy: Harlequin Books is committed to protecting your privacy. Our Privacy Policy is available online at www.eHarlequin.com or upon request from the Reader Service. From time to time we make our lists of customers available to reputable third parties who may have a product or service of interest to you. If you would prefer we not share your name and address, please check here. ☐

TWO CROWNS, TWO ISLANDS, ONE LEGACY

A royal family, torn apart by pride and its lust for power, reunited by purity and passion

coming in 2009

BILLIONAIRE PRINCE, PREGNANT MISTRESS
by Sandra Marton, July

THE PLAYBOY SHEIKH'S VIRGIN STABLE-GIRL
by Sharon Kendrick, August

THE PRINCE'S CAPTIVE WIFE
by Marion Lennox, September

THE SHEIKH'S FORBIDDEN VIRGIN
by Kate Hewitt, October

THE GREEK BILLIONAIRE'S INNOCENT PRINCESS
by Chantelle Shaw, November

THE FUTURE KING'S LOVE-CHILD
by Melanie Milburne, December

RUTHLESS BOSS, ROYAL MISTRESS
by Natalie Anderson, January

THE DESERT KING'S HOUSEKEEPER BRIDE
by Carol Marinelli, February

8 volumes to collect and treasure!

HP12835

Life is a game of power and pleasure.
And these men play to win!

THE SHEIKH'S LOVE-CHILD
by *Kate Hewitt*

When Lucy arrives in the desert kingdom of Biryal,
Sheikh Khaled's eyes are blacker and harder than
before. But Lucy and the sheikh are inextricably
bound forever—for he is the father of her son....

Book #2838

Available July 2009

Two more titles to collect in this exciting miniseries:
BLACKMAILED INTO THE GREEK
TYCOON'S BED by *Carol Marinelli*
August

THE VIRGIN SECRETARY'S
IMPOSSIBLE BOSS by *Carole Mortimer*
September